LUCIFER AND THE ANGEL

A warm wave of fragrance and sunlight greeted them as they crossed the room to the orchids.

"I told you, Anita," said the Duke, "never come to a Conservatory alone with a man unless you want him to make love to you."

Her eyes widened. "I . . . I never . . . thought . . ."

". . . that it applied to me?" the Duke finished. "Well, it does! That is why, my darling, I brought you here—to tell you that I love you!" He swept her into his arms, claiming her lips with his, filling her with joy that was like the sun coming through the clouds . . . and like Heaven. . . .

Bantam Books by Barbara Cartland
Ask your bookseller for the titles you have missed

Barbara Cartland's Library of Love series

Books of Love and Revelation

Other books by Barbara Cartland

Lucifer
and
the Angel

Barbara Cartland

LUCIFER AND THE ANGEL
A Bantam Book / September 1980

ISBN 0–553–13942–8

Published simultaneously in the United States and Canada

Bantam Books are published by Bantam Books, Inc. Its trade-
mark, consisting of the words "Bantam Books" and the por-
trayal of a bantam, is Registered in U.S. Patent and Trademark
Office and in other countries. Marca Registrada. Bantam
Books, Inc., 666 Fifth Avenue, New York, New York 10103.

PRINTED IN THE UNITED STATES OF AMERICA

0 9 8 7 6 5 4 3 2 1

Author's Note

"One would think the English were ducks; they are for ever waddling in the waters," said Horace Walpole in 1750.

The origins of British Spas date back to Roman times, when the thermal waters at Bath were used for bathing.

In the early Eighteenth Century there were 228 Spas in England and Wales. Today there are few which still have a medical reputation for healing. The most important is Harrogate, which averages annually 120,000 treatments.

The usual crosses of the martyrdom at a Spa had to be borne at Harrogate according to reports published in 1822. When new arrivals met the famous sulphur-waters for the first time—hot, stinking, and fizzing—they surreptitiously hid in corners to spit it out.

Later, one of *Punch's* anonymous rhymsters, 'Arry at 'Arrygate, reported:

Reg'lar doctor shop 'Arrygate is; see their
photos all over the town;
Mine is doing me dollops of good, I'm quite
peckish and just a bit brown.
I'm making the most of my time, and laying in
all I can carry,
So 'ere ends the budget of brimstone and baths,
from your Sulphur soaked 'Arry.

I stayed in Harrogate some years ago when I visited Harewood House, the home of the Princess Royal who married the Earl of Harewood. Built in 1759, Harewood House is a treasure-store of works of art and is now open to the public.

Chapter One

1860

Anita stood against the gate and looked across the field to the little wood where she so often sat when she wanted to be alone to think.

She had actually put her hand out towards the latch when, looking up, she saw the clouds which had been grey and heavy all day suddenly part and a brilliant shaft of sunlight shine down towards the earth.

Instantly there came to her mind the text she had heard yesterday from the pulpit.

It was a somewhat unusual one for the Reverend Adolphus Jameson to have chosen, and it had attracted Anita's attention when, anticipating one of his long, erudite, and incredibly boring discourses, she was already slipping away into her dream-world.

"'*How are thou fallen from Heaven, O Lucifer, son of the morning!*'" the Reverend Adolphus had boomed out.

Instantly Anita had a picture of the handsome Archangel falling and deing deprived of "*everlasting bliss.*"

His expulsion from Heaven had always fascinated her, and now staring at the sunlight she wondered what Lucifer had looked like before he had sinned.

She had a vision of his face, handsome, smiling, and yet with perhaps even in the celestial regions a somewhat raffish glint in his eyes, as if his fate was

1

already decided for him before the final act which sent him hurtling down to perdition.

Then abruptly, breaking in on her reverie so that she started, a voice asked:

"Well, young woman, are you going to open the gate for me or continue daydreaming?"

She turned round and gave a gasp, for there behind her, seated on a magnificent black stallion, was Lucifer himself, just as she had always envisaged him.

She was looking at his face, which was handsome but undoubtedly cynical and disillusioned, his dark eyes mockingly accentuated by his raised eye-brows, and even the high silk hat set on the side of his dark head seemed appropriate in place of the halo of light which had once been his.

If she was bemused by the gentleman's appearance he was also surprised by hers.

He had thought, seeing a woman or a girl alone, standing beside the five-barred gate which led to the pasture on which he wished to ride, that presumably she came from a nearby farm.

But the small, heart-shaped face with its large blue eyes and the soft, very pale hair which curled round an oval forehead belonged to no milk-maid, and he thought too that the girl was very young, perhaps still in her teens.

Because she was staring at him in a bemused fashion, a faint smile curved the corners of his rather hard mouth and he asked:

"Of whom were you dreaming in such an absorbed fashion?"

Almost as if she was compelled to answer him, Anita replied:

"Of Lucifer!"

The gentleman laughed.

"And now you think you see the Prince of Darkness in person?"

Since this was the truth she was not surprised, but she had no reply and after a moment he said:

"If you knew your poets you would be aware that *'The stars move still, time runs, the clock will strike, the devil will come.'*"

He recited the lines as if they were familiar, and as he finished Anita said softly:

"Christopher Marlowe."

"So you do know your poets!" the gentleman remarked. "Well, beware of Lucifer wherever you may find him! That is the best advice I can give you."

He glanced away from her as he spoke, and, as if she suddenly remembered why he was there, she undid the latch on the gate and at her touch it swung open.

"Thank you," the gentleman said, "and remember what I have told you."

He smiled as he spoke, as if he thought it unlikely that she would do so.

Then he cantered away, moving swiftly towards the end of the field, and she thought as she saw him go that he *"went into the darkness of the damned."*

Slowly, still watching him far in the distance, Anita shut the gate, knowing that she had now no wish to visit her secret wood. She would rather go home and think of the stranger she had met, who undoubtedly resembled Lucifer.

She longed to tell somebody of her strange encounter, but she knew only too well that her sisters, Sarah and Daphne, would laugh at her.

They always mocked her over-active imagination and the dreams which made her oblivious to everything that was going on round her.

"But this dream was real!" Anita told herself. "He was really there, Lucifer, Son of the Morning!"

It was strange that he looked exactly as she had envisaged him: the lines running from his classical nose to the corners of his mouth, the faint shadows underneath his eyes, his lips that she felt could speak bitter and cruel words although he had merely sounded cynical.

3

*"When he falls, he falls like Lucifer, never to
hope again."*

She had learnt the words from Shakespeare's
Henry VIII with her Governess, but she thought they
were not appropriate for the Lucifer on the black
stallion who was obviously not repentant of his fall
and not without hope.

Then, remembering Christopher Marlowe, whom
he had quoted, she thought of two lines that described him exactly.

It was Mephistopheles who said:

*O by aspiring pride and insolence,
For which God threw him from the face of heaven.*

Pride and insolence—that was what she felt her
Lucifer, the one who had spoken to her, had.

Walking back to the Manor, she thought of a
dozen things she wanted to say to him, a hundred
questions she would have liked to ask.

Then she told herself that he would have thought
her crazy. He was in fact only a gentleman, undoubtedly a guest of the Earl of Spearmont, whose parties
were the talk of the village and of everyone in the
County.

'I shall never see him again,' Anita thought as she
reached the Manor, 'but I shall always remember
what he looked like.'

* * *

"Good-bye, Mama!"

"Have a lovely time, we will be thinking of
you!"

"Please write as often as you can."

"Good-bye . . . Good-bye!"

The girls were still repeating the same words as
the rather old-fashioned but comfortable carriage carrying their mother and the Squire's wife, Lady Benson, started down the drive.

They watched till it was out of sight, then went
back into the shabby hall which somehow seemed

empty after being filled only a moment earlier with loving farewells and last-minute instructions.

"Now that Mama has gone," Sarah said, "I want to speak to you, so come into the School-Room."

Daphne and Anita followed her into the room which, even now when they were all grown up, was still called the School-Room, although Mrs. Lavenham had done her best to make it a cosy Sitting-Room where they could keep their own particular belongings.

There was the easel which Daphne used for sketching and a miscellaneous collection of paints and brushes.

There was Sarah's sewing-basket, which was very like her mother's, and Anita's books which filled a whole bookcase and, despite innumerable protests, were piled untidily on the floor.

The sofas and chairs were covered in slightly faded but pretty chintz that matched the curtains.

There were flowers on the table and the sunshine coming through the window made it a very happy room.

Sarah stood on the hearth-rug and waited until Daphne and Anita had seated themselves before she said:

"I have been thinking about this for a long-time."

"About what?" Daphne asked. "And what do you want to speak to us about?"

"That is what I am trying to tell you," Sarah said impatiently.

She was the most spectacular of the three sisters, and her pink-and-white skin, her golden hair with red lights, and her hyacinth-blue eyes had proclaimed her a beauty before she had left the School-Room.

"You must have a Season in London and somehow you must be presented at Court," Mrs. Lavenham had said over and over again, and Sarah had looked forward to it and had been as sure as her family were that she would be a success.

Then disaster had come. Her father, the Honourable Harold Lavenham, had a fall out hunting.

5

His horse had rolled on him and he had been badly injured.

There had been two long years of pain before finally he died, and now when the year of mourning was over, the Doctors had discovered that the strain of it had affected his wife to the point where they suspected she had a patch on her lung.

"Six months in Switzerland could save your mother's life," the Doctors had said firmly.

They had all thought that such expense was impossible, until the Squire's wife, Lady Benson, who had always admired their mother, had offered not only to take her to Switzerland but to stay with her for at least three months of her time there.

She had been unwell too, but for a different reason, and it seemed not only an excellent arrangement from Mrs. Lavenham's point of view but also a God-send in that they would only have to find one fare and pay for one person in the Hotel where she was to stay for her treatment.

But they were aware that almost all the money that was available would be spent on their mother and there would be little left for those who stayed behind.

Both Daphne and Anita guessed that this was what Sarah meant to talk about now, and they looked at her a little apprehensively.

Sarah was very much the head of the household even when their mother was there.

She was a born organiser, and since her father's death she had undertaken to handle their small finances and prevent the over-spending he had never been able to avoid when he was alive.

"As you are both aware," Sarah began, "I thought that I might be obliged to accompany Mama to Switzerland and I was in fact dreading that I should have to do so."

"It might have been interesting to see a foreign country," Daphne remarked.

"Interesting!" Sarah exclaimed derisively. "The place where Mama has gone is full of elderly invalids,

6

and in the brochure it says the Doctors insist there are no diversions or amusements that might tempt their patients from following diligently the strict routine of the cure."

"Oh, poor Mama!" Anita said sympathetically.

"Mama will not mind," Sarah replied. "She is determined to get well, and besides, she will have Lady Benson to gossip with. But there would have been no-one of my age."

The sharpness of her tone made her sisters look at her in surprise, and Sarah went on:

"Do you two realise that I am nearly twenty-one? And I have never been to a Ball except for the local ones, which do not count. I have never had my Season in London. I have never done anything but wait on Papa and Mama and look after you!"

Before Anita could speak, Daphne gave a little cry.

"Oh, Sarah, I never thought of that! How selfish we have been! But Papa was so ill, and when he died Mama was so unhappy."

"I know," Sarah said dully, "and I have done my best—I really have done my best."

"Of course you have, dearest," Anita agreed.

Daphne jumped out of her chair to put her arms round Sarah and say:

"You have been an absolute brick and we all know it!"

"I do not want your praise," Sarah said. "Sit down, Daphne, I want to tell you what we are going to do."

She paused as if she was feeling for words. Then she said:

"I have already written to Papa's sister, the Countess of Charmouth, asking her if she will have me to stay."

"To Aunt Elizabeth?" Daphne exclaimed. "But she has never paid any attention to us and never even came to the Funeral when Papa died."

"I am aware of that," Sarah replied, "and we

7

know that Papa's family did not approve of his marrying Mama, but there is no reason why they should disapprove of us."

"The Countess has never invited us to anything," Daphne persisted.

"Never, but she will find it very hard to refuse what I have suggested in the letter I have written to her."

"What have you suggested?" Anita enquired.

"I have asked her if I can come and stay with her for the last two months of the Season. I explained that Mama has had to go to Switzerland and that as we are left alone here, we are appealing to her, as one of our few remaining relatives, to show some compassion to Papa's eldest daughter because, if he were alive, he would have been so grateful."

Sarah made what she was saying sound very appealing, and Daphne gave a little laugh as she said:

"You are right, Sarah, I feel she cannot refuse to do what you ask."

"That is what I am hoping," Sarah said, "and that your Godmother, Lady de Vere, will have you."

Daphne gave a little gasp.

"My—Godmother? But she has not written to me or sent me a present since I was confirmed."

"I know that," Sarah replied, "but she is very rich, and although she is getting old she entertains a lot in what Papa said was a magnificent house in Surrey."

"I remember his telling us about it," Daphne said.

"I wrote her very much the same letter as I wrote to Aunt Elizabeth, and because I am sure she always had a tenderness for Papa, I feel she will agree to have you."

Daphne clasped her hands together.

"I do hope so!"

"So do I," her sister replied.

Sarah's eyes now rested on Anita.

As she did so, she was thinking how very young she looked.

Anita was in fact just eighteen, but as she was so small and had a face like a flower and the look of a small cherub, she seemed little more than a child.

"What about me?" Anita asked as Sarah did not speak. "Am I to stay here alone with Deborah?"

"I have not forgotten you, Anita," Sarah said in a softer tone than she had used hitherto, "but we have run out of relations, except for one."

"Who is that?"

"Great-Aunt Matilda."

For a moment Anita looked puzzled, then she said:

"We have not heard from her for so long! Are you sure she is still alive?"

"I think so. She certainly was when Papa died, because she sent a wreath to the Funeral."

"I had no idea of that!" Daphne exclaimed. "But then, there were so many."

"If you remember, I made lists of who sent them and wrote and thanked everybody."

"Where does Great-Aunt Matilda live?" Anita asked.

"The wreath was sent from Harrogate," Sarah replied. "It came by post and was made of leaves, which I thought very sensible, for flowers would have died on the journey."

"Do you think Great-Aunt Matilda will want me?" Anita asked in a small voice.

"I daresay she will not want you any more than Aunt Elizabeth or Lady de Vere will want Daphne and me," Sarah answered, "but I intend that they shall take us. You do realise, girls, that this is our great chance and, as far as I am concerned, the last."

She saw that Anita at any rate had not understood, and she explained:

"To find ourselves husbands! Surely you are aware that if we stay here, living as we have done for the last three years, we shall all die old maids?"

As her voice seemed almost to ring out in the School-Room, both Daphne and Anita were aware that Sarah was speaking the truth.

9

In the little village of Fenchurch, where they lived, there were no young people of their own age, and after their father's death it appeared that they had been forgotten by the County families, of which there were not many.

It was Sarah who realised only too clearly that nobody wanted three girls without a man to escort them and, what was more, three girls who were outstandingly attractive.

The Squire, Sir Robert Benson, and his wife invited them frequently to luncheon and dinner, but Sir Robert was over sixty. His son, already married, was serving with his Regiment in India, and his daughter had chosen a life of seclusion as a Nun.

The most spectacular and talked-of house in the County belonged to the Earl of Spearmont, but he and his wife belonged to the smart set that circled round the Prince and Princess of Wales at Marlborough House and they said openly that they "never entertained the locals."

The people who lived near them had to be content with the gossip that was repeated by the servants, or to catch an occasional glimpse of beautiful women and handsome men as they rode or drove in smart carriages through the village.

Sarah was right.

In their way of life since their father's illness and death there had been no opportunities of meeting eligible bachelors, and where Sarah herself was concerned the position was growing desperate.

She was in fact so pretty that it was not surprising that she yearned for a wider and more appreciative audience than her mother and sisters and the Squire and his wife.

"What we have to decide now," she was saying, "is how much we can afford to spend on new clothes, which are very necessary unless we are to appear like creatures out of Noah's Ark."

"Clothes!" Daphne ejaculated almost ecstatically.

"I do not suppose I shall need anything at all

smart in Harrogate," Anita said. "From what I re-member Papa saying about Great-Aunt Matilda, she is given to 'good works,' and I am therefore not likely to meet a prospective husband with her, unless he is in Holy Orders!"

Sarah laughed. Anita had a funny way of saying things which they all found amusing.

"Do not worry, dearest," she said. "If I can marry someone of importance or at least wealthy, both you and Daphne can come and stay with me, and I will scour London and the countryside, or wherever I may be living, for every eligible bachelor."

"Of course, that is the solution!" Daphne ex-claimed. "So you must have the beautiful clothes, Sa-rah, and Anita and I will manage somehow."

She sounded a little wistful because she had often imagined how exciting it would be to have gowns that had not been passed down to her after Sarah had grown out of them.

"What I am hoping," Sarah said, "is that your Godmother, who I believe is very wealthy, will not only have you to stay but will provide you with the type of clothes you will need as her guest."

"I can hardly ask her to do so!" Daphne exclaimed.

"No, of course, not," Sarah answered, "but I did point out in my letter how poor we are and how we had been very fortunate in being able to send Mama to Switzerland, and then only with the help of her friend Lady Benson."

Anita moved a little uncomfortably.

"It does sound, Sarah, as if we were begging."

"Of course it does!" Sarah said sharply. "And so we are! Make no mistake about it, we are beggars, and I am not ashamed to say so. After all, the Laven-ham family owes us something."

"Owes us?" Daphne asked.

"But of course!" Sarah replied. "They behaved abominably when Papa married Mama, simply be-cause Grandpapa, being an Earl, was puffed up with pride in his own consequence. He thought even his younger son should marry someone with a title or

11

money, and Mama had neither. But she was exceedingly beautiful and Papa fell in love with her."

"The moment he saw her," Anita said dreamily, "it was just like a story in a book. And Mama said that as soon as she looked at Papa she knew he was the man she had always seen in her dreams."

"It was certainly very idyllic," Sarah said, "but we each want to find the man of our dreams too, and we are certainly not going to meet him or any other sort of man here."

Anita wanted to reply that, strangely enough, she had met a man only that morning, and he was Lucifer.

Then she knew that Sarah would be annoyed at anything which interrupted her recital of her plans.

When Sarah was concentrating on something she expected everybody else to do the same, so Anita went on listening as Sarah told them what money was available for them to spend and what arrangements she had made for the house to be taken care of while they were away.

"You are very sure the relatives you have written to will have us?" Daphne asked at length in a low voice.

"They have to! They have to do what I have asked them to do," Sarah said, and now her voice was desperate. "Otherwise, I feel we are all doomed!"

* * *

The Duchess of Ollerton, sitting in the window of the large house she had rented in Prospect Gardens, felt that the sulphur-baths and the chalybeate waters she was drinking every morning were doing her some good.

She had come to Harrogate because, after listening to what her Doctor had to say on the subject of her health, her son had insisted that she should do so.

She found it impossible to protest that she had no wish to leave the comfort and beauty of her own house to travel North.

She had learnt since she became a widow that it

was useless to oppose her son once he had made up his mind, especially where it concerned her.

He had certainly arranged everything to make her as comfortable as possible.

The house, which had been chosen by his Secretary and Comptroller, was large and extremely well furnished and belonged to an aristocrat who had gone abroad for the summer.

It contained practically everything that a Lady of Quality would need, but when the Dowager Duchess of Ollerton travelled, she moved, as someone had once said laughingly, "like a snail with her house on her back!"

She had therefore travelled from the South with her own linen, her own silver, and of course her own servants. Besides this, there were also what Her Grace was pleased to describe as "knick-knacks."

There alone filled a large number of trunks and required several carriages to transport them from the Duke's private train to the house in Prospect Gardens.

Among the many things without which the Duchess never travelled was a portrait of her son, Kerne, now the fifth Duke of Ollerton.

It stood on a large easel, which had been made especially for it, not far from where the Duchess was stitting, and her eyes softened as she looked at the Duke's handsome face and thought how well the artist had portrayed his dark eyes and firm chin.

Almost as if her very thoughts of him had conjured him up, the door opened and he came into the room.

The Duchess held out her hands with a little cry.

"You have arrived, dearest! I was hoping it would be today, but Mr. Brigstock thought it was more likely to be tomorrow."

"As you see, it is today," the Duke said. "How are you, Mama?"

He reached her side as he spoke and bent down to kiss the softness of her cheek, holding one of her hands in both of his as he did so.

"I am better, I really am better," the Duchess said, "and looking forward to going home."

"You have not been happy here?"

There was a faint frown between the Duke's eyes as he spoke.

"It has been an interesting experience," the Duchess answered, "but quite frankly not one I wish to repeat. You know as well as I do that I hate to be away from Ollerton and from you."

"I too have missed you, Mama."

"It is so very sweet and kind of you to come and see me," the Duchess said.

The Duke released her hand to sit down in a chair opposite her.

"I will be honest, Mama, as I know you would wish me to be, and tell you that although I was eager to see you again, my journey North was not solely a filial duty."

"You had another reason?" the Duchess asked, smiling. "Let me guess—I feel it has something to do with the Earl of Harewood and his superlative horses."

The Duke laughed.

"You are always intuitive where I am concerned, Mama. Yes, it is true. When I leave you I will be staying at Harewood House before I go on to Doncaster for the races."

"Have you a horse running?" the Duchess enquired.

"Three, as it happens," the Duke replied, "and I think one of them will definitely win the best race."

The Duchess sighed.

"How I wish I could be there."

"Perhaps next year, Mama. But if you are well enough, perhaps you could manage one day at Ascot."

"It is something I would most enjoy," the Duchess smiled, "and I am sure Her Majesty would be gracious enough to have me to stay at Windsor."

"You know she would," the Duke replied, "but

you must be well enough. All that standing in the Royal Presence might be too much for you."

"It might indeed," the Duchess agreed. "But tell me more about your visit to the Marquis of Doncaster. I have always found him a very charming man."

"So have I," the Duke said, "and that is why you will understand, Mama, that I am interested in meeting his daughter."

There was a moment's silence and the Duchess was very still. Then she said:

"Do you mean—can you be—thinking—?"

"Of marriage," the Duke said, finishing the sentence for her. "Yes, Mama. I have come to the conclusion that it is time I was married."

"Oh, Kerne, it is what I have prayed for!" the Duchess exlaimed. "But is it Marmion who has made you decide so suddenly that it is something you should do?"

"It is Marmion," the Duke agreed, "but more directly the Queen."

"The Queen?"

"Her Majesty spoke to me last week."

"About Marmion?"

"That is right."

The Duchess made a little sound that might have been one of horror, but she did not interrupt.

"Her Majesty asked me to speak with her in her private Sitting-Room. I knew at once that what she had to say was serious."

"It was also likely to be only one subject," the Duchess said quickly.

"Exactly! She told me she had heard that Marmion and his wife were in a Box at Covent Garden the night the Prince of Wales was there and they were both behaving in what the Queen described as an 'outrageous manner.'"

"I presume Her Majesty meant that they had both had too much to drink," the Duchess said in a low voice.

"I heard from another source that they were disgracefully, revoltingly drunk!"

"Oh, Kerne, what can we do about it?"

"There is nothing we can do," the Duke replied, "except to make sure that Marmion does not inherit the Dukedom after me."

"And is that what Her Majesty said?"

"She pointed out to me," the Duke answered, "that the Duchess of Ollerton is traditionally a Lady of the Bedchamber."

"And of course Her Majesty could not countenance that vulgar creature whom your cousin has taken as a wife in that capacity," the Duchess added.

"That is exactly what Her Majesty implied," the Duke said, "and so, Mama, the time has come, regrettable though it may be, that I must be married."

"Of course, dearest, but must it be regrettable?"

The Duke waited a moment before he said:

"I have no wish to be married, Mama, as I have told you when we have discussed the subject many times before. I am entirely content as I am, but I am well aware that it is my duty to provide an heir to the Dukedom. I therefore need your help."

"My help?" the Duchess echoed in surprise.

The Duke smiled.

"With the exception of the Marquis's daughter who happens to be the right age—and the last time I visited Doncaster she was still in the School-Room—I am not in the habit of meeting young girls, and in none of the houses in which I stay do they feature among the guests."

"No, of course not!" the Duchess exclaimed. "I understand that."

"So, what I am asking you to do, Mama," the Duke went on, "is to make a short list of the girls you think are eligible, and I will look at them before deciding on the one I think most suitable."

The Duchess said nothing, and, looking at her, the Duke asked:

"What is wrong, Mama? I thought that you, of all people, after all you have said about my being mar-

16

ried and producing a son, would be delighted that the moment has come when that is exactly what I mean to do."

"Of course I am delighted that you should be married, Kerne dear," the Duchess replied, "but I had hoped, perhaps foolishly, that you would fall in love."

The Duke's lips twisted wryly.

"That is what the servants would call 'a very different kettle of fish.'"

"But your way seems such a very cold-blooded manner in which to get married."

"What is the alternative? You have met most of the charmers—and I am not pretending there are not a number of them—who have engaged my heart for a short period, but none of them is eligible to become my wife."

The Duchess, who knew a great deal more about her son's love-affairs than he imagined, admitted to herself that this was true.

His *affaires de coeur*, though conducted very discreetly, were nevertheless common knowledge amongst the society in which he moved, and the Duchess had friends who were only too willing to tell her the latest gossip.

She was therefore aware that for the last six months the Duke had been constantly in the company of an acclaimed beauty whose husband was quite prepared to ride His Grace's horses, sail in his yacht, drink his wine, and turn a "blind eye" to his host's preoccupation with his wife.

This, the Duchess thought was very civilised behaviour, an example which had been set by the Prince of Wales.

But there was no doubt that the Duke was correct in saying that at the house-parties at which he was either a guest or a host there was no likelihood of a young, unmarried girl being present.

As if he knew what his mother was thinking, he bent forward to say:

"Do not look so worried, Mama. When I am married I promise you I will behave with great propriety towards my wife. But she must be exactly the right person to take your place, although no-one could ever look as beautiful as you."

He spoke with such sincerity that the Duchess put out her hand to him as she said:

"Dearest Kerne, you have been a wonderful son to me, and I hope that your wife, whoever she may be, will appreciate you. At the same time, a marriage needs love, and that is what I would wish you to find."

As if embarrassed by the turn of the conversation, the Duke rose to his feet.

"Love is one thing and marriage is another, Mama. Let us concentrate on marriage. Find me the right sort of wife, one who must of course grace the Ollerton diamonds."

The Duchess smiled.

"That means, as the tiaras are higher and more magnificent than anyone else's, that she must be tall."

"Of course," the Duke agreed. "At least five-foot-nine or -ten, and because the sapphires always look their best on fair women, she should have hair the colour of ripe corn."

The Duchess said nothing, but her eyes twinkled a little as she remembered that the last three women with whom the Duke's name had been associated were all brunettes.

"Then, of course, there are the pearls," the Duke continued, following his own train of thought. "Five rows of them, Mama, need someone with, shall we say, a full figure, to show them off."

" 'Junoesque' is the right word, dearest," the Duchess said. "It is a description I have always enjoyed myself, and you will remember that until I was afflicted by this terrible rheumatism, I managed to keep a very small waist."

"I am not likely to forget it," the Duke said. "Somebody was saying only the other evening that their idea of beauty was you blazing with diamonds and wearing a long train standing at the top of the staircase at Ollerton House."

"You are always very complimentary, dearest," the Duchess said, "and I love it! I know exactly what your wife should look like, but it will not be easy to find her."

The Duke walked across the room and back again.

"God knows, Mama," he said after a moment, "it is going to be difficult not only to find the type of wife that I require, but also to endure her once I have done so. What does one talk about to an unfledged girl?"

"There is no woman born who is not interested in love," the Duchess said softly.

The Duke made a derisive sound, but before he could speak she went on:

"You should remember, dearest, that the beauties you now find so desirable were once unfledged girls straight from the School-Room. They all start out that way—gauche, shy, ignorant, and uneducated."

"God knows it is a dismal prospect!" the Duke exlaimed.

The Duchess laughed.

"It is not going to be as bad as that! I admit I was shy when I married your father, and I suppose in many ways I was very ignorant. But, although we were brought together by our parents because it was considered a suitable marriage, I made your father very happy."

"You know as well as I do, Mama, that Papa fell head-over-heels in love with you from the moment he saw you. He told me once you were the most beautiful thing out of a stained-glass window he had ever seen in his whole life."

The Duchess smiled complacently while her son went on:

"But Papa added: 'They do not make them like that these days, Kerne,' and he was right!"

"I made your father happy and that was all that mattered," the Duchess said. "There is no reason why we should not find a woman just like me to do the same for you."

The Duke sat down again next to his mother.

"Papa loved you whole-heartedly, Mama, until he died. What about you?"

For a moment the Duchess looked at him with startled eyes, then she asked:

"What do you mean by that?"

"Exactly what I say. Papa was much older than you, and although it was an arranged marriage it turned out, as far as he was concerned, to be a perfect one. But did you fall in love as whole-heartedly as he did?"

Again there was silence, and the Duchess looked away from her son.

"Love, when one finds it," she said after a moment, "is so wonderful, so perfect, that one would never regret it."

"I think you have answered my question," the Duke said. "But it is not really an answer to my problem. You see, Mama, I have never known the kind of love which Papa felt for you and which you have obviously found in your life, if not with him."

The astonishment in the Duchess's eyes was very obvious, and without her having to ask the question the Duke said:

"I know, I know! There have been women in my life ever since I was at Eton, and it seems a strange thing to say, but always sooner or later, generally sooner, they have been disappointing."

"Kerne, dearest, I am so sorry!"

"There is no need to be," the Duke said. "They have given me a great deal of pleasure and amusement, but I have often asked myself, Mama, when I remember what Papa felt about you, if I am missing something."

"Oh, dearest, I thought you had everything!" the Duchess cried.

"That is what I have wanted to believe," the Duke answered, "but when I am being honest, as I am now with you, I know it is not quite true. Then I tell myself I am asking too much."

The Duchess looked at him with great tenderness in her eyes.

She had always known he had a desire for perfection above that of any other man she had ever known.

In everything he did, everything he possessed, the Duke had to excel.

His houses had to be better than anybody else's, his servants more efficient, his horses had to win all the classic races, his shoots had to achieve the highest bag of the Season.

The women he squired were undoubtedly the outstanding beauties of the moment, and now it was understandable, she thought, that there could be one thing which he might find was not perfect.

Just as she was about to say something, the Duke gave a little laugh as if he mocked himself.

"I am becoming maudlin, Mama. You know as well as I do that I am reaching for the moon, and no-one as yet has touched it."

"Perhaps one day . . ." the Duchess said softly.

"No, no, do not let us delude ourselves," the Duke answered. "Let us be practical and go back to the moment when I asked your help. I want a wife, Mama, and I am asking—no, indeed, I am commanding you to find me one who will answer all my requirements, but let me make one thing clear."

"What is that?" the Duchess asked.

The Duke paused for a moment as if he was choosing his words.

"I do not want a woman who is over-demonstrative. Her character must match her appearance. She must be conventional, dignified, and emotionally controlled. That is what I will expect from my wife and the Duchess of Ollerton."

"But, Kerne . . ."

"No 'buts,' Mama. As we have already agreed, marriage and love are two different things and I have no wish to try to combine them in a way which I know would undoubtedly prove a failure."

Chapter Two

As she walked towards the Pump Room Anita looked round her with delight.

She had not expected Harrogate to be so pretty, and she had in fact been extremely apprehensive as she and Deborah had journeyed North in the train which carried them to a terminus in West Park.

The letters that Sarah had written so diligently had all received prompt replies.

The Countess of Charmouth wrote that she would be delighted to entertain her niece for the rest of the Season and would send a carriage to collect. her, complete with an elderly maid to chaperone her on the journey.

What was even more practical, she sent Sarah some money to buy a new gown and bonnet in which to travel, and she wrote:

> *Everything else, my dear niece, can wait until you arrive, and I am quite certain from what you have told me in your letter that you will require a whole new wardrobe with which to appear in Society. I am looking forward to seeing you and I so often think of your dear father and the happy times we had when we were children.*

"Nothing could be kinder than that!" Sarah exclaimed in triumph.

"No, indeed," Daphne agreed, "and my Godmother's letter is very pleasant too, although she apparently expects me to find my own way to London, and from there she says a Courier will escort me to her house in Surrey."

"That means," Sarah replied, "that Deborah will have first to take you to London, then travel with Anita to Harrogate."

The letter written by Great-Aunt Matilda was not only very much less effusive than those which Sarah and Daphne had received, but enclosed with it was only the fare for two Second Class tickets to Harrogate.

"Second Class, indeed!" Deborah snorted indignantly when she was told how they had to journey. "And her as rich as one of them Indian nabobs they're always talking about in the papers!"

"How do you know that?" Anita enquired.

"I remember your father telling your mother about his Aunt Matilda, and saying she was a miser, while any money she did spend was to ensure herself a good place in Heaven, if she ever reached it!"

Anita laughed. She was used to Deborah's sharp remarks and her familiarity.

She had nursed them all as children and was now getting old, but she still managed in an amazing way to keep the house clean and to bully them into doing all the things their mother would have expected them to do.

"It will be an exciting adventure to go by train to Harrogate," Anita said, as if she was anxious to appease the elderly woman.

"You should be travelling First Class, Miss Anita, and I've a good mind to tell Miss Lavenham so when I sees her."

"Oh, please, Deborah, do not do anything of the sort!" Anita begged. "She might be so angry that she will send me back right away, and then I should have to stay here alone, and Sarah would be extremely annoyed."

"Miss Sarah's all right, God bless her. She's picked herself the juiciest plum in the pudding, and let's hope something comes of it."

Deborah spoke in the voice of one who would be

23

surprised if it did, but Anita knew she was afraid that their desperate adventure would come to nothing and that when the winter arrived they would all be back in the Manor House, skimping and saving and having no-one to talk to but themselves.

Not that Anita would mind.

She could always escape into her daydreams, especially now that she had a very special one to dream about, and that was Lucifer.

The more she thought about him sitting astride the black stallion, the more she was beginning to be convinced that he was entirely a figment of her imagination.

How could any real man look so exactly like the fallen Archangel that the most skilful artist in the world could not have drawn him more accurately?

"I dreamt him! I know I dreamt him!" Anita said to herself.

Then she remembered the dry, sarcastic note in his voice as he said:

"Beware of Lucifer, wherever you may find him!"

If he was really Lucifer, Anita thought, he would not be warning her against himself.

She had spent many hours wondering what wickedness the Devil actually did when he was behaving as was expected of him.

There must be other vices besides pride and insolence, but she had no idea what they could be.

The books she had read in her father's Library, while they certainly improved her mind and added to her knowledge, were not very explicit as to what constituted "sin."

Although the Reverend Adolphus spoke of it frequently, he never added any informative details which Anita often thought might have been interesting.

The gentleman had, however, given her many new ideas to think about and many more dreams to dream.

It was true that the girls were very limited with regard to relatives. Their grandfather, the Earl of

Lambourn and Beckive, had three sons but they had all died without producing an heir for the Earldom.

The present and ninth Earl was therefore a very distant cousin, who lived in South Africa and had sold the family Estates.

Anita had often wished that he would invite them to visit him, but even if he did so, she knew they could not afford the expensive fare.

But now she was travelling, if only to Harrogate, and all the way in the train, having been fortunate enough to obtain a corner-seat, she stared out at the countryside, trying to decide which County she was in.

She thought they should really be divided by fences in brilliant colours which would make it easy to distinguish between them!

There was flat land, meadow land, forests, valleys, and dales before finally the train steamed into Harrogate and they were there.

"This is thrilling, Deborah!" she exclaimed when they took an open hackney-carriage to carry them through the town to Great-Aunt Matilda's house.

"Don't go expecting too much. Miss Anita," Deborah replied. "You'll only be disappointed, and you've got to remember that Miss Lavenham is very old and I don't suppose she's much idea of what young people like."

She snorted and added:

"I'd have thought Miss Sarah could have found you a better place to go."

Anita had heard all this before, but she said gently:

"I am afraid we have very few relations left alive, and as I am the youngest it is only right that I should wait my turn."

To her surprise, Deborah gave her one of her rare smiles.

"You never knows what mightn't turn up, Miss Anita, even in a place like Harrogate, where you'll find most people have one foot in the gravel"

Anita laughed. Then as the carriage began to slow down she said in a low voice:

"I do wish you were staying with me, Deborah. It would be fun if we could be together."

"I'd like that too," Deborah replied, "but I'm afraid Miss Lavenham will be thinking that I'm one more mouth to feed."

That, Anita found later, was exactly what she did think.

She had already formed a picture of what Great-Aunt Matilda would look like and she had not been far away from the truth.

Mrs. Lavenham was old, and yet able to sit stiffly upright in her chair, despite the rheumatism which prevented her from walking.

She wore on her grey hair a white muslin cap which was exactly like the pictures of the one worn by Queen Victoria.

She did in fact look very like Her Majesty, except that her face was thinner and more lined and had, Anita thought apprehensively, an undoubtedly grim appearance.

"So you are my youngest niece!" she said in a deep, gruff voice when Anita was announced. "You are very small, and not in the least like your father!"

She made it sound a very regrettable failing, but Anita smiled at her bravely and made the speech she had already rehearsed.

"How do you do, Great-Aunt Matilda, and thank you very much for having me to stay with you. It is very kind."

"Your sister left me very little choice," Miss Lavenham remarked accusingly, "but now that you are here, I daresay you can make yourself useful."

"I hope so," Anita answered, "but in what way?"

"You will soon learn. What about this servant you have brought with you? She can stay tonight, but she will leave tomorrow on the morning train."

Anita hesitated a moment, then she said:

"It would be kind if she could stay just a little

longer. It was a tiring journey, and Deborah is not as young as she was."

"She can rest in the train," Miss Lavenham replied in a voice which told Anita that the subject was closed.

So Deborah went back and Anita quickly found that there were a lot of things for her to do.

Miss Lavenham was indeed given to good works, as her father had said, and there were dresses to be made which were straight plain shifts called "Mother Hubbards." They were sent out to the Missionaries in Africa to clothe those who were ignorant enough to walk almost naked.

There were tracts to be addressed and delivered to hundreds of people who lived in Harrogate or in the vicinity, either by Anita or one of the servants in order to save the postage.

There were also collections that were made for all sorts of strange charities which Anita had never heard of before.

She soon learnt that the only people who came to the house regularly were those connected with the religious organisations that Great-Aunt Matilda patronised.

Her own personal Minister, the Reverend Joshua Hislip, was a frequent visitor because, as Anita soon surmised, he never left empty-handed.

Fortunately, Anita learnt the very day after her arrival that Great-Aunt Matilda's health compelled her to drink the waters.

This meant that early every morning they went to the Cheltenham Pump Room.

Miss Lavenham was pushed there in a bath-chair by an elderly footman, and Anita walked beside her, her eyes delighted with everything she saw, especially the people who were journeying in the same direction.

Some were very smart and made her conscious of how out-of-date her own clothes were.

Sarah had looked lovely setting off for London in

27

a new travelling-gown with a large crinoline and a cloak which swung out over it.

Daphne had a new bonnet, but there had been nothing left to spend on Anita. She had, however, bought some yards of blue ribbon to trim the bonnet she had worn for two years.

Although she had not realised it, her blue gown, made by Deborah, with its gleaming white muslin collar and cuffs, made her look very young, very innocent, and more than usually like a small angel.

She was wearing it now and her blue eyes were alight with interest as she followed Great-Aunt Matilda's bath-chair in through the gate.

The Cheltenham Pump Room was the largest public building in Harrogate and had a most impressive Doric-columned portico which reminded Anita of Roman Architecture.

Inside was a large Salon where the invalids congregated to gossip, a Pump Room, and a Library to which fortunately Miss Lavenham subscribed.

Having lived in Harrogate all her long life, she knew practically everybody in the town and looked on it as if it were her own personal property and Estate.

Anita found that Great-Aunt Matilda regarded newcomers with a jaundiced eye and was on the defensive in case any of them, through ignorance, encroached on the privileges which she thought were her right.

Like all old people, she disliked change and wanted everything that happened today to be exactly the same as it was yesterday, the day before that, and back through the years.

She therefore expected her bath-chair to come to rest regularly at the same point inside the Pump Room.

Almost every morning there was a battle because some unwary person who had just arrived in Harrogate had encroached on the actual spot that Miss Lavenham considered to be hers and hers alone.

Anita found that Great-Aunt Matilda had a very scathing tongue, and she felt herself blushing at the rude things the old lady would say, even though the newcomers would quickly make their apologies and withdraw from the sacred unmarked patch on which they had unwittingly trespassed.

When Anita had been there two or three days, she realised that the men who pushed the bath-chairs that were for hire often deliberately took up their position on Miss Lavenham's piece of floor, just for the fun of it.

When they had been forced to retreat she would see them laughing and winking at one another, and she wondered how it could matter so much to Great-Aunt Matilda that she was prepared to make what her father would have called "an exhibition of herself."

However, Anita was clever enough to realise that her Great-Aunt was an eccentric, and, as such, the town in its own way was rather proud of her.

As soon as her bath-chair, which was a very comfortable one with a thickly padded seat, was in the correct position, Anita would be sent to the well.

There she obtained a glass of mineral-water, which had special properties in it, especially iron, and which had brought invalids to Harrogate since 1571 when the waters were first discovered.

Anita had already found a book which described the chalybeate Tewit Well, whose waters *"did excel the tart fountains beyond the seas as being more quick and lively and fuller of mineral salts."*

She thought personally that the waters tasted rather nasty and felt fortunate that, being so well, she did not need it.

This morning, looking round at the many invalids crowded into the Pump Room, she decided to say a little prayer that they might all recover after they had drunk from the well.

The idea made her imagine what a commotion there would be if suddenly all those who were sipping from the glasses their attendants had brought them were suddenly to jump up from their bath-chairs and cry out in amazement that they were cured.

Then she told herself that in that case they would undoubtedly sing a hymn of joy and gratitude, and she could almost hear the Hallelujahs that would rise in a paeon of triumph towards the high ceiling of the Pump Room.

She was thinking how exciting this would be, when a glass of mineral-water intended for Miss Lavenham was held out to her by the attendant at the well.

She took it in both hands, and, still thinking that it might constitute a miraculous cure, she turned round rather swiftly.

As she did so, she stumbled over the foot of the bath-chair that was just behind her and with a little cry half-fell across it, spilling the contents of the glass she held in her hand.

She picked herself up and looked in consternation at the lady in the bath-chair.

"I am sorry ... I am very ... very ... sorry," she apologised. "It was clumsy of me. I do hope I have not hurt you, Ma'am?"

"No, I am all right," a sweet voice replied, "and perhaps we were too near to the well."

"I do hope the water has not spoilt your rug," Anita said, looking down to where there was undoubtedly a wet patch on the pretty paisley rug which covered the lady's legs.

She found her handkerchief and was bending down to wipe it dry when a voice she remembered only too well remarked:

"I think once again you must have been dreaming, but I cannot believe this time it was of Lucifer."

Startled, she looked up and there, standing behind the bath-chair, was in fact Lucifer.

He looked exactly the same as he had when they had met before and as she had visualised him almost every day since.

The only difference was that he was standing instead of riding, while his tall hat was still at a rakish angle on his dark head and his coat fitted as elegantly across his broad shoulders.

She stared at him wide-eyed. Then the lady in the bath-chair said:

"You appear, Kerne, to have an acquaintance with this young lady already. Perhaps you would introduce me?"

"We met by chance, Mama, and as she told me, she was at that moment thinking of Lucifer, I think perhaps I am connected in her mind with that particular gentleman."

The Duchess looked at her son in surprise, then said to Anita:

"Will you tell me who you are?"

A little late Anita remembered to curtsey.

"I am Anita Lavenham, Ma'am," she answered, "and I am staying in Harrogate with my Great-Aunt Miss Matilda Lavenham."

"Matilda!" the Duchess exclaimed. "Good gracious, is she here?"

"She is over there on your right," Anita replied, "and please, if you will excuse me, I must fetch her another glass of water."

She curtseyed again hesitatingly and hurried back to the well while the Duchess said to her son:

"I should have thought Matilda Lavenham was dead years ago, but let us go and speak to her. I remember her when I was a girl, and I suspect that your young friend is the daughter of that very handsome nephew of hers, Harold Lavenham."

Back at the well, Anita had waited her turn for another glass of the mineral-water, and when finally she received it, she carried it very much more carefully to her Great-Aunt, to find that the lady in the bath-chair over whom she had fallen was talking to her.

Standing a little apart from them both and looking rather cynical and bored was Lucifer.

"You have been a long time, Anita!" Miss Lavenham said sharply as she took the water from her hand.

"I am sorry, but I had to wait," Anita replied.

As she spoke she gave the Duchess a glance to

see if she would betray her, but she received an encouraging smile. Then Miss Lavenham said in a manner which seemed almost reluctant:

"This, Clarice, is my great-niece, Anita. You may remember her father?"

"Of course I remember Harry Lavenham," the Duchess replied. "He was the most handsome man I ever danced with, and I used to follow him out hunting, knowing he would always be in at the kill."

"Those were the days when he could afford to hunt with a decent pack," Miss Lavenham replied.

Anita knew that once again she was referring to the fact that everything that was luxurious in her father's life had come to an end when he married not a rich bride, as was expected of him, but her mother.

Ever since Anita had arrived in Harrogate, Great-Aunt Matilda had made it very clear that the circumstances in which her great-nieces found themselves at this particular moment were due entirely to their father's profligate life.

Anita knew it would have been quite useless for her to point out that her father had been so happy with her mother that he had never missed any of the advantages he had enjoyed when he had lived at home.

She knew only too well that Great-Aunt Matilda would not understand that love was a compensation for everything else that her father could no longer afford.

She was wise enough to suspect that because Great-Aunt Matilda had obviously never been in love she was inclined not only to disparage that emotion but also to consider it an unnecessary luxury for everybody else.

Now for the moment it was difficult to concentrate on what Great-Aunt Matilda was saying or indeed of whom she was speaking.

Instead Anita found herself vividly conscious that Lucifer's dark eyes were on her face, and she wondered what he would say if she asked him how long he intended to stay away in the Hell he had recently chosen instead of Heaven.

With a faint smile to herself she thought that not only he would be astonished if she said such a thing, but doubtless Great-Aunt Matilda would send her home on the next train for being impertinent.

"I wish I had known you were here before, Matilda," the Duchess was saying. "I have been in Harrogate for five weeks and it would have been pleasant to talk of old times."

"I am too busy to entertain," Miss Lavenham answered sharply, "but if you would care to visit me for a dish of tea next Sunday you will be very welcome."

"Thank you," the Duchess replied. "If I am able, I shall be delighted, and I hope you and your niece will come to me before I leave. I have rented Lord Arrington's house on Prospect Gardens and find it extremely comfortable."

"A ridiculous man who worries far too much about his health!" Miss Lavenham sniffed. "When he told me he was visiting the Spas in France and Switzerland I informed him it was a waste of money."

As she spoke, she signalled the footman who was pushing her chair to take her away, and at the same time handed her empty glass to Anita.

Quickly Anita returned it to the side of the well where a great number of other used glasses had been deposited.

Then as she turned to hurry after her Great-Aunt, who by now had left the Pump Room, she found that she had to pass by Lucifer.

He blocked her passage and she was forced to stop.

"Are you taking my advice, Miss Lavenham?" he enquired.

She knew to what he was referring, and that, knowing what she thought of him, he was mocking her.

33

"I remember what you said, Sir," Anita replied, "but you forget you also told me that 'the Devil would come.' I am therefore apprehensive as to how I can stop him."

She saw the amusement in his eyes at her reply. Then, without waiting for him to speak, she ran from the Spa, catching up with Great-Aunt Matilda, whose bath-chair was already moving swiftly out through the gates onto the road.

They proceeded for quite some way before Miss Lavenham said:

"I presume you know who those people are?"

"No," Anita replied, "you introduced me to them but you did not tell me their names."

"That was the Dowager Duchess of Ollerton," Miss Lavenham said, "and her son. A frivolous man, from all I have heard, but that might be said of any young man today."

Anita did not reply.

She had already heard, a number of times, her great-aunt's opinion of modern youth and their lack of responsibility.

What did interest her was that Lucifer was the Duke of Ollerton.

Anita had always thought that Dukes were old, pompous, and overpowering. The Duke of Ollerton was certainly the latter, but he was not pompous.

He had a lithe grace about him which had made her imagine he could easily have glided down from Heaven with his wings outstretched, landing with an athletic ability which prevented him from hurting himself.

The Duke of Ollerton!

It sounded a very formidable title, and now she could no longer think of him just as Lucifer but as a nobleman, and she was quite certain that somewhere she had heard his name before.

It took her a long time to remember where, until she recalled that her father had liked her to read the newspapers to him when he was ill, and that included the reports of race-meetings.

Of course, the Duke was amongst those who owned winners of great races including the Derby and the Gold Cup at Ascot.

"Papa would have liked to meet him," Anita told herself.

Then she wondered if he would come to tea with his mother on Sunday when her Great-Aunt had invited the Duchess, but she thought that if he did he would be considerably bored.

She had learnt that usually the only guest was the Reverend Joshua Hislip, and last week there had been two ladies who had devoted their lives to teaching sign-language to children who were born deaf and dumb.

It was all very worthy, Anita knew, but she was quite certain that the Duke of Ollerton would not find it particularly entertaining.

"No, he will not come," she told herself, and wondered if she would ever see him again.

❋   ❋   ❋

In the large Drawing-Room of the house in Prospect Gardens, the Duchess, when she had been seated comfortably in her favourite place in the window, said to her son:

"That was a pretty child with Matilda Lavenham, but I cannot imagine she has much of a life. Matilda is obsessed with the needs of the poor and the needy in every country but her own."

"I could see she was an old battle-axe!" the Duke remarked. "But I imagine the girl is only with her on a visit. When I saw her before it was in Cambridgeshire."

"Was Anita staying with the Earl of Spearmont?" the Duchess asked.

"Good Lord, no!" the Duke replied. "I was riding and asked her to open a gate for me, thinking she was a milk-maid, but she was daydreaming and she told me she was thinking about Lucifer."

"So that accounts for your extraordinary conversation with her," his mother remarked.

35

Barbara Cartland

The Duke seated himself in a comfortable chair, and after a moment the Duchess said:

"As you asked me, Kerne dearest, I have made a list for you. It is not a very long one."

She drew out from a silk bag beside her a piece of paper, but as she held it out to him the Duke said:

"There is no need for me to read it. Invite the girls, if you think they are any good, to stay at Ollerton in three weeks from now. I will give a party at which, Mama, you will preside, and although it will be a crashing bore, I suppose I must do my duty."

"We shall have to ask their fathers and mothers," the Duchess commented.

"Of course," the Duke agreed, "and I will include a few friends of my own to cheer up what will undoubtedly be a laborious few days of utter boredom."

The Duchess drew in her breath.

"I hate you to talk like that, Kerne," she said after a moment. "You must remember, dearest, it is your future we are planning, and once you are married there will be nothing anyone can do."

The Duchess spoke a little hesitatingly, and the Duke said:

"I am well aware of that, Mama, but as we have agreed that Marmion and his appalling wife must not on my death inherit Ollerton and all the responsibilities that go with my position, however unpleasant it may be, I must make the best of a bad job."

"I have chosen girls whose parents are an example of propriety," the Duchess said, "and what is more, I know Her Majesty will approve of them."

"Then I can only say thank you, Mama, and beg you to stop worrying about me, as you are doing at this moment."

"Of course I worry. What mother would do anything else in the circumstances?"

"Perhaps it will not be as bad as we both anticipate," the Duke said, "and I am sure, Mama, that, if nothing else, you will think it is very good for my soul. You have accused me often enough of being spoilt and selfish."

"Not where I am concerned," the Duchess said quickly. "You have never been anything but kind and very unselfish to me, and however much you may deny it, that is why you are here at this moment, boring yourself in Harrogate of all places."

"As a matter of fact I am finding it quite amusing," the Duke replied. "Apart from being with you, the Earl of Harewood has told me I can use the excellent horses he has at Harewood House as if they were my own, and I am trying out a team this afternoon. I only wish you were well enough to come with me."

"I wish I were too, dearest," the Duchess replied. "When you return, tell the Earl I hope he and his wife will call on me before I leave. I have not been well enough to drive over to Harewood to leave my cards with them."

"I am sure they will wish to come and see you."

The Duke rose as he spoke and bent down to kiss his mother's cheek.

"You are looking much better, Mama," he said, "and I think we can thank Harrogate for that."

He would have moved away but the Duchess held on to his hand.

"Before I send out the invitations, dearest," she said, "you are quite, quiet certain that this is what you wish me to do?"

"Quite certain," the Duke said firmly, "but because it bores me I do not wish to discuss it any further."

"No, of course not," the Duchess said, releasing his hand.

There was, however, a deep sadness in her eyes as she watched him walk from the room and close the door quietly behind him.

*　　*　　*

Three days later, the Duke, driving a team of four perfectly matched chestnuts, turned a corner of the road and saw a small figure running swiftly ahead of him along the pavement.

He thought he recognised the blue ribbons of the bonnet he had last seen in the Pump Room, and it surprised him first of all to see that Anita was alone and unaccompanied, and secondly that she should be running away from the town in the same direction as the one in which he was driving.

He was aware that Cornwall Road, once it had passed Knaresborough Forest, would take him out to the open countryside and it was there that he intended to test the speed of the horses which he was driving so that he could report on their progress to their owner.

He pulled his horses in until they were level with the small figure moving surprisingly quickly, then brought them to a standstill.

Anita must have been aware that he was trying to attract her attention, for she turned her face towards him and he saw that her eyes were filled with tears and they had spilled over onto her cheeks.

"You appear to be in a great hurry, Miss Lavenham," the Duke remarked drily. "Perhaps you would find it easier to travel more swiftly, wherever you are going, in my chaise."

"I ... I am ... going to the ... country," she replied after a moment, a little incoherently.

"As that is also my destination," the Duke said, "it is obvious that we should journey together."

He put out his left hand as he spoke, and, almost as if he commanded her to do so, she took it and stepped into the chaise to sit down beside him.

She made no effort to wipe away her tears, and after he had started his horses again the Duke asked:

"What has upset you?"

"I ... I want ... to go ... h-home ... I want to ... g-go away," Anita said. "B-but I have ... no money ... and I am not sure that I can ... do so."

"What has occurred to make you feel like this?"

For a moment he thought she was not going to

answer him. Then, because he was waiting and she felt she must reply, she said in a voice that broke:

"Great-Aunt Matilda has told me that I am to m-marry the ... Reverend ... Joshua ... H-Hislip."

"And the idea upsets you?"

"He is ... old ... and he is ... always preaching about ... the punishments that await those who ... sin ... and when he looks at me ... I think there is ... f-fire in his eyes."

The Duke thought somewhat drily that perhaps the Reverend Joshua had fire in his eyes for a very different reason than Anita's sins, but aloud he said:

"Surely if you do not wish to marry him it is quite easy to say 'No'?"

"Great-Aunt Matilda tells me that it is my ... duty because his wife has died and he needs ... somebody to look after him," Anita replied. "Sarah said we were all to find husbands ... but I cannot marry him ... I think I would rather ... die!"

There was no doubt of the despair in Anita's voice, but the Duke merely asked:

"Who is Sarah?"

"My sister. When Mama went to Switzerland, Sarah wrote to our relations, who had paid no attention to us before, asking them to have us to stay. She thought it was our last chance to find ... ourselves husbands. There are no ... young men where you first saw me in ... Fenchurch."

"So you are husband-hunting?" the Duke said and he made it sound a very unpleasant pursuit.

"Sarah is nearly ... twenty-one," Anita explained, "and she cannot wait. But I have plenty of time, and anyway ... I have no wish to ... marry anyone ... unless I ... love him!"

Her voice broke on a little sob.

Then, as if for the first time she realised that her face was streaked with tears, she put up her fingers to her cheeks before beginning to search for a handkerchief.

As she seemed regrettably to have omitted to

bring one with her, the Duke took the square of fine linen from his breast-pocket and handed it to her.

As she turned her face to thank him, he thought she cried like a child.

The tears were running down her cheeks whilst her eyes were still wide open and swimming with them, and he knew that he had never known a woman who could cry so prettily without contorting her face.

"Thank...you," Anita faltered. "You will think I am very...foolish...but somehow I know that Great-Aunt Matilda will...force me to...marry the Reverend Joshua because she thinks him such an... admirable man."

"Your father is dead," the Duke said, "but I cannot believe you do not have some nearer relative who could be constituted as your Guardian and to whom you could appeal for help?"

"There is only the Countess of Charmouth, my Aunt Elizabeth, who is Papa's sister," Anita said. "Sarah is staying with her and it would not be...fair for me...to interfere."

The Duke, being concerned with his horses, did not speak, and she went on:

"I...I must run away...if I can go home... perhaps I could hide so that Great-Aunt Matilda could not make me return to her...and the Reverend Joshua could not...find me."

She twisted her fingers together for a moment before she said in a very small voice:

"B-but I have...no m-money."

"So you are asking me to lend you some," the Duke said.

"C-could you? Please...could you do that?" Anita asked. "I promise you I will return it...every penny. It might take a long time...but you shall have it back."

"If I give you money," the Duke said, "what exactly would you do with it?"

"I will find out what time the train leaves for the South," Anita replied, "then I will creep out of the house and be gone before anyone realises it."

"Do you really think you can travel alone? All the way back to Fenchurch, if that is the name of your village?"

"Yes ... that is right," Anita said, "and I do not think the ... Second Class fare is very expensive, or if you prefer ... I will go Third."

"I would prefer you to do none of those things. We have to think of some alternative."

"There is none," Anita said quickly. "When Great-Aunt Matilda told me after luncheon before she went to lie down that I was to ... marry the Reverend Joshua, she said he was ... coming to see me ... to-morrow. That means I must go ... tonight."

"But where were you running to now?" the Duke asked.

"I have always found it easier to think when I am in the country," Anita replied simply. "Somehow it is much more difficult in the town where there are houses and people moving about. I thought I would find a wood, like the ... secret wood I go to at home, where I could sort ... things out in my ... mind."

"Is that where you went after we first met?"

Anita shook her head.

"No. I went ... home."

"Why?"

"I was ... thinking about you ... because I thought you were ... Lucifer. It was so interesting and exciting that it was unnecessary to think in my wood."

The Duke smiled before he said:

"Because it looks as if it may rain later on this afternoon, I suggest I do not leave you in Knaresborough Forest, which I see we are approaching, but we think out your plans while you are with me."

"I have told you ... I must go ... home," Anita said.

"If your sisters are away, will there be anybody there?"

"There is Deborah, our old maid. She is taking care of the house until Mama is well enough to come back from ... Switzerland."

41

"It does not seem a very satisfactory arrangement," the Duke remarked. "There is also, of course, the chance that you may not get away."

Anita gave a little cry.

"But I have to...I have to! If the Reverend Joshua comes to see me tomorrow, I know that however much I may...insist that I will not...marry him, Great-Aunt Matilda will...make me do so. Why should he want me? There must be many other women—the Church was full of them on Sunday—who would wish to be his wife. It is ridiculous for him to want me!"

The Duke looked sideways at her small cherub-like face and her large worried eyes.

He thought of quite a number of reasons why the Reverend Joshua should wish to marry her apart from the fact that it obviously had the approval of his most influential patron.

Because he had no wish to make Anita more frightened than she was already, he merely said:

"You are quite certain it will not be in your best interests to be married? After all, if, as you say, Fenchurch is so dull, you might find life in Harrogate considerably more entertaining."

"Not with...that man as my...h-husband," Anita said in a whisper. "When he...shakes my hand it makes me...creep and I feel as if he were a... snake. How could I let him...touch me?"

There was such a note of horror in her voice that the Duke almost instinctively tightened his hands on the reins. Then he said:

"I am now going to drive very fast, and when I have tried out these horses perhaps we shall find a solution to your problem."

He did not wait for her answer but cracked his whip and the horses sprang forward, moving quicker, Anita thought, than she had ever travelled before.

The dust from the road billowed out behind them and she thought that she was not travelling with Lucifer but with Apollo as he drove his chariot across the sky, carrying the light from one side of the world to the other.

It made her thrill at the sheer excitement of it, then when they were approaching the end of the straight part of the road the Duke slowed his team down and a few minutes later turned them round.

"That was exciting!" Anita said. "And the horses are superb! Where did you find them?"

"They are not mine, as it happens," the Duke said, "but I have horses of my own which can travel as fast as these, if not faster, although I admit it would be hard to fault them."

"Then please do not try to do so," Anita begged.

"Why not?" the Duke enquired curiously.

"Because it is always so disappointing to find that something we thought was perfect falls short of our expectations."

"You are too young to have found that out already," the Duke remarked, and there was a distinctly cynical note in his voice.

"So we must never expect too much," Anita said, as if she was talking to herself, "but try to be grateful that it is as good as it is."

"The way you are speaking," the Duke remarked, "I feel you would make an excellent Parson's wife."

She gave a cry of horror.

"That is unkind, and cruel of you! You are only saying that to ... hurt me! I was not sermonising, but I am really trying to work out in my own mind why you should be cynical when as a Duke you must have everything you want in the world ... and a great deal more ... besides."

The Duke laughed.

"Who has been telling you tales about me?"

"Not you in particular," Anita replied, "but Dukes are very important people ... I know that ... and because they are next in line to Royalty one wants to believe they are happy."

The Duke laughed again.

"You are making me the Duke in a fairy-story,

43

one of those tales you tell yourself when you are
looking at the sky or collecting waters from the Spa."

"How do you know I do that?" Anita asked.

"It is obvious."

"I try not to do it . . . all the time."

"I think it would be a mistake to change yourself," the Duke remarked. "Small angels obviously
believe that everything is perfect."

He smiled again before he quoted:

" *'Now walk the angels on the walls of Heaven, as
sentinels to warn th' immortal souls.'* "

He saw Anita look at him with a sudden light in
her eyes and asked:

"Is that what you are doing?"

"Is that what . . . you are . . . telling me I . . . do?"
she enquired. "Do I really look like an angel?"

"Exactly!"

"It is a lovely idea," Anita said almost to herself.

"So what could be more appropriate than to be
warning his immortal soul when you are driving with
Lucifer?"

"I suppose it was . . . impertinent of me to think
you . . . looked like him," Anita said. "It is just that
when you appeared I was thinking how handsome he
must have been before he fell from Heaven."

The Duke thought he had been paid many compliments in his life, but this was the most ingenu-
ous.

"Thank you," he said, and saw a quick blush
come into Anita's cheeks.

"Perhaps I should not have . . . said that," she
murmured. "The things I think sometimes pop out
without my really considering them, so you must
forgive me."

"There is nothing to forgive," the Duke said, "and
now as we are turning homeward I think I have a
solution to your problem."

"You have?"

Now there was a very different note in Anita's
voice as she clasped her hands together.

She turned sideways, looking up at him, her eyes beseeching him.

"Do you really mean, Your Grace, that you will help me? Please ... please ... if you will do so I will be ... grateful all my life!"

"I will certainly try to do so," the Duke said. "And I think that you will not be disappointed."

"Promise that I will not have to ... marry the ... Reverend Joshua!"

"Not unless you wish to do so."

"You know that can be never ... never ... never!" Anita cried. "But how can you ... prevent it?"

"I think we shall have to have somebody else's help," the Duke said.

Then, as he saw the expression of concern on Anita's face, he added:

"Do not look so worried. The person to whom I am referring is my mother!"

Chapter Three

The Duchess was sitting in her favourite seat in the window when to her surprise she saw her son driving back towards the house.

As he had left her well over an hour ago to return to Harewood House, she could not imagine what had made him return.

She waited, and when she heard his footsteps outside the room she looked up expectantly.

He came in, but before he could speak she cried:

"What has happened, Kerne? I did not expect to see you again so quickly!"

"It is nothing to upset you, Mama," the Duke replied as he walked over to her side.

"Then what is it?" the Duchess enquired.

The Duke sat down in a chair next to her before he answered:

"While I was driving I saw Miss Lavenham's great-niece and found her in great distress."

"What can have upset her?"

"Apparently," the Duke said, "your old friend, who you tell me is given to good works, has decided that the child should marry her pet Minister."

The Duchess looked astonished.

"You cannot mean the Reverend Joshua Hislip?"

"I believe that is his name."

"But he is old, and a most unpleasant man as far as I am concerned. When I listened to him last Sunday he was literally mouthing over the punishments the wicked would suffer for their sins, and I had the feeling it was something he would enjoy inflicting personally if he had the chance."

"Then you will understand, Mama," the Duke said, "that it would be criminal to let that young girl be forced to marry someone who is old enough to be her father."

"I believe somebody told me that the Reverend Joshua's wife died fairly recently," the Duchess said. "But of course he is much too old for Matilda's great-niece—what did she say her name was?"

"Anita."

"At the same time," the Duchess went on, "there is nothing I can do about it, and I am quite certain Matilda Lavenham would greatly resent my interfering in any way."

There was silence for a moment, then the Duke said:

"I thought, Mama, that you needed a Reader."

The Duchess started indignantly.

There was nothing on which she prided herself more than that her eyes, unlike those of most of her contemporaries, were exceedingly good. She could see for a long distance, and, what was more, she needed to use a magnifying glass only for the very smallest print.

She was just about to say that a Reader was the last thing she needed, when, as the words came to her lips, she bit them back and instead, after a distinct hesitation said tentatively:

"If you really—think that is what I—require, Kerne, then I am sure you are—right."

"I thought you would agree with me, Mama," the Duke said, "and as you are leaving for home tomorrow, I think you would find it agreeable to have someone to read the newspapers to you on the long journey."

"Are you suggesting that Anita Lavenham should come with me?" the Duchess enquired.

"It would be best if she came here tonight," the Duke replied, "for I understand the amorous Parson will press his suit tomorrow at midday."

"Then of course that must be prevented," the Duchess agreed. "What do you suggest I do?"

"I have already ordered the carriage for you, Mama. I think if you drive to Miss Lavenham's house and ask her, as a favour, to lend you her niece, she will be unable to refuse."

"Yes, of course, dearest," the Duchess said. "Perhaps you will ring for Eleanor to bring me my bonnet and shawl."

The Duke rose to his feet to pull the bell, and the Duchess watched him with an astonishment that he did not perceive.

It was true that she had often accused him of being selfish and there had been many people who said he was spoilt because he had been a much-cosseted only child.

The Duchess thought that in the years since he had grown up he had never shown the slightest interest in other people's problems.

"Now I will set off once again for Harewood House," the Duke was saying, "and I hope to have no more adventures on the way. Tomorrow I repair to Doncaster, and I shall be at Ollerton in about two-weeks' time."

"I have invited your guests to stay with us from the twenty-fifth," the Duchess said.

"Thank you, Mama. And of course Brigstock will go back in the train to look after you during the journey and see that you have everything you require."

"I am sure Mr. Brigstock will do that admirably," the Duchess replied.

She held out her hands.

"Good-bye, dearest boy. Enjoy yourself at the races, and I hope your horses win."

"I shall be extremely annoyed if they fail."

The Duke kissed his mother and hurried away as if he was anxious to be once again driving the chestnut horses that were waiting for him outside.

As she saw his broad shoulders disappearing

through the door the Duchess murmured beneath her breath:

"A Reader indeed! But I suppose it is as good an excuse as any other!"

* * *

Anita, having hurried back on the Duke's instructions to her great-aunt's house, found that she was in for a scolding for having been away so long.

"There is plenty for you to do here, Anita," Miss Lavenham said severely, "without gallivanting off on your own, which is something of which I do not approve."

"I am sorry," Anita answered humbly. "It was a nice day and I walked farther than I intended."

"This craze for exercise amongst young people is quite unnecessary," Miss Lavenham snapped, "especially when they are neglecting their duties. Hurry up and finish those letters so that you can give them to the Vicar when he calls tomorrow."

She did not notice that Anita gave a little shiver when she thought of the real reason why the Reverend Joshua was calling the following day.

Already she was beginning to wonder frantically whether the Duke would keep his word and save her from what she thought would be a fate too horrible to contemplate.

It was all very well for Sarah to talk of their finding husbands, but Anita's vivid imagination had already made her realise that having a husband entailed more than just bearing a man's name and looking after his house.

What exactly it was, she had no real knowledge. She knew only that the idea of the Reverend Joshua touching her or kissing her was horrible and unnatural.

When she had seen him in the pulpit the first Sunday after she had arrived, she had thought him an ugly, boring man.

Accordingly, she had drifted away into one of her

daydreams, which strangely enough concerned Lucifer, although the Reverend Joshua's sermon in no way
resembled the one given by the Reverend Adolphus:

*"How are thou fallen from Heaven, O Lucifer,
son of the morning!"*

Anita repeated the words to herself and thought
with a little smile that her Lucifer had fallen very
comfortably into the position of a Duke.

When the Reverend Joshua had called later that
afternoon for tea with her Great-Aunt Matilda, she
had thought him even more unpleasant at close quar-
ters than when he was officiating in the Church.

There was something smarmy and certainly slimy
in the way he talked to her Great-Aunt, and Anita did
not miss the glint of what she was sure was greed in
his eyes when, as he was leaving, Miss Lavenham had
handed him a sealed envelope.

"Just a little donation to your favourite charity,
my dear Vicar," she had said in a surprisingly soft
voice.

Anita thought that perhaps she was being unjust,
but she had a suspicion that the Reverend Joshua's
favourite charity would be himself.

He called very frequently, and it struck Anita the
following Sunday that he held her hand in his wet
and clammy one rather longer than was necessary.

She also heard him saying complimentary things
about her to her Great-Aunt Matilda.

"If he knew what I thought about him," she had
told herself, "he would sing a very different tune!"

However, she had not thought of him more than
she could help, and this morning she had been preoc-
cupied and excited by the first letter she had received
from Sarah, who had written:

*I cannot tell you how wonderful it is being
in London with Aunt Elizabeth, and she has been
kinder to me than I thought possible. The
clothes she is giving me are lovely, so lovely
that every time I put them on, I feel I am*

Cinderella and my Fairy Godmother has waved her magic wand over me.

Fancy I have an enormous crinoline and already there are four ball-gowns hanging in my wardrobe besides a number of absolutely ravishing other dresses!

I want to tell you, darling Anita, about the Balls I have attended and the Reception at which Aunt Elizabeth actually presented me to Princess Alexandra, but I have no time now as I have to get ready for a large luncheon-party.

I hope you are not too unhappy at Harrogate and I will write again as soon as it is possible. This is really just to tell you that I love you and wish you were here with me.

Anita read the letter over and over again. She told herself that Sarah was so lovely that everybody would admire her and she was sure she would find exactly the husband she desired.

She spent the morning daydreaming about Sarah and it was therefore a shock when, as luncheon ended, a plain, rather dull meal, Miss Lavenham said:

"I wish to speak to you, Anita, before I go for my rest."

Anita looked surprised, but she followed her great-aunt into the Morning-Room which was adjacent to the Dining-Room.

When they shut the door her great-aunt said:

"Sit down, Anita. I have something to tell you which I am sure, will make you realise what a very fortunate girl you are."

It flashed through Anita's mind that her aunt might be going to give her a new gown, but Miss Lavenham went on:

"You have met the Reverend Joshua Hislip here a number of times and listened to him in Church. You must realise he is a man of outstanding ability and character."

She paused, and because it was obviously expected that Anita should reply, she said:

"Yes, indeed, I am sure he is."

"You will therefore appreciate," Miss Lavenham continued, "what a very great honour it would be to become his companion and wife."

It struck Anita with a sense of some surprise that if her great-aunt wanted to marry, it was certainly strange that she should take such a step when she was over seventy.

But when she considered it, she was sure the Reverend Joshua would find it very much to his advantage to have such a wealthy wife.

Also, there was no doubt that Great-Aunt Matilda was extremely fond of him.

Aloud she said:

"So you are to be married, Great-Aunt Matilda! How very exciting! Will I be able to be your bridesmaid?"

There was a moment's stony silence when Anita realised she had said something wrong.

Then, anunciating every word so that there would be no mistake, Miss Lavenham said:

"The Vicar has asked for *your* hand in marriage, Anita!"

Despite the way she spoke, Anita felt she could not have heard her aright. Then with a little cry she exclaimed:

"N-no ... but he cannot have! How ... could he? He is much too old!"

"Age is of no consequence," Miss Lavenham replied sharply, "and as the Vicar has said himself, you will bring him the spring when he has existed for so long in the cold and snows of December."

Because for a moment Anita was incapable of speech, Miss Lavenham continued:

"He was referring to the fact that his wife was ill for a number of years before she died. Personally, I always found her a tiresome woman, possessive and querulous, and she failed to give him children, although that might have been an act of God."

"Child ... ren!"

Anita whispered the words beneath her breath.

Then bravely, because her heart was thumping in her breast, she said:

"I am sorry ... Aunt Matilda ... but I could not ... marry any man who is ... so much older than I am ... and someone I did not ... love."

Miss Lavenham brushed her words aside as if they were no more important than the buzzing of a mosquito.

"Nonsense! Nonsense!" she said. "Of course you will marry the Reverend Joshua, and think yourself extremely lucky to do so. You will not have a big wedding. That would be quite unnecessary. I will give a small Reception here, and I presume I shall have to supply your trousseau."

Anita rose to her feet.

"No! ... No! ... I cannot ... and I will not ... marry the Reverend ... gentleman!"

"You will do as you are told!" Miss Lavenham retorted. "I have no wish for him to be disappointed and the marriage has my full approval. I presume, as your father is dead and your mother is abroad, that I as the eldest of the Lavenham family, am in the position of being your Guardian, and as your Guardian, Anita, I will have no opposition to my plans. When the Vicar calls tomorrow you will accept him and I shall make arrangements for you to be married in a month's time."

The way Miss Lavenham spoke was so positive, so overpowering, that Anita felt as if the walls were closing in on her and there was no escape.

With a little cry like that of an animal caught in a trap, she hurried from the room and ran upstairs to her bedroom.

She had locked herself in, and when she heard her Great-Aunt come upstairs to lie down, she had put on her bonnet and slipped out of the house, feeling that only outside the town, in the country, could she breathe and think.

Then the Duke had providentially met her and promised he would rescue her, but how he could do so she had no idea.

She was just now thinking despairingly that she would have to run away tonight and somehow find her way home to Fenchurch when the Butler opened the door to announce:

"The Duchess of Ollerton, Ma'am!"

Miss Lavenham looked surprised but Anita felt her heart leap.

The Duchess walked very slowly and obviously with some difficulty towards Miss Lavenham, who rose to her feet.

"What a surprise, Clarice! I was not expecting you."

She helped the Duchess into a chair, who did not reply until she was comfortable. Then she said:

"I feel very remiss in not calling before, Matilda, and as I am leaving tomorrow this is my last opportunity of paying my respects. Moreover, I want to ask you a great favour."

"I had no idea you were leaving so soon," Miss Lavenham interposed.

"It has been quite a long visit," the Duchess replied. "I am sure the sulphur-baths have done me good, and I certainly feel better for having taken the waters."

"I am very glad to hear that."

Listening, Anita thought her Great-Aunt always behaved as if a compliment to Harrogate was also a compliment to herself.

She had risen from the desk at which she had been writing and now the Duchess smiled at her.

"You appear to be very industrious, my child."

Anita curtseyed.

"Yes, Your Grace. I am writing letters for an appeal which Great-Aunt Matilda is sending out on behalf of the Missionaries in West Africa."

"How kind you are," the Duchess said to Miss Lavenham, "and of course you must let me contribute."

"There is no need," Miss Lavenham replied, but added quickly: "Although, of course, every penny counts."

The Duchess opened her reticule, which hung from her wrist.

"Here are five sovereigns," she said, "and I hope my contribution does all the good you expect it to."

"The natives in West Africa have been sadly neglected," Miss Lavenham said, taking the golden sovereigns which the Duchess held out to her. "The Reverend Joshua Hislip whom you heard preach on Sunday, hopes we shall be able to send our own Missionary from Harrogate to save their souls by converting them to Christianity."

As Miss Lavenham spoke the Reverend Joshua's name, the Duchess was aware that Anita was looking at her with a desperate plea in her blue eyes.

"I actually came to ask you, Matilda," the Duchess said, "as a very great favour, if you would lend me your niece."

"Lend you my niece!" Miss Lavenham exclaimed with an incredulous note in her voice.

"I am travelling home tomorrow in my son's private train—a new acquisition of which he is very proud," the Duchess explained. "But it is still a long journey, even if it will be in comparative comfort—and, my eyes not being what they were, I would so much appreciate having somebody to read to me."

Anita drew in her breath and she thought for one moment from the expression on her Great-Aunt's face that she was intending to refuse.

Then Miss Lavenham said with obvious reluctance:

"It would be difficult for me not to lend you Anita in the circumstances. At the same time, I would wish you to send her back here as soon as you have no urgent need of her."

"But of course!" the Duchess replied. "I realise how much she means to you, Matilda, and it is exceedingly kind of you to let me have her, as my son is unavoidably prevented from taking me home himself."

"At what time do you wish Anita to be with you?" Miss Lavenham asked.

"I think it would be most convenient if she came with me now," the Duchess replied. "I am sure that while you and I have a cup of tea together, Matilda, and talk over old times, she will be able to get her things packed, and my carriage is waiting outside."

There was a distinct pause before Miss Lavenham agreed to this suggestion, and Anita thought frantically that she was considering sending for the Reverend Joshua to talk to her before she left.

"If that is what you want, I suppose I must agree," Miss Lavenham said abruptly.

Then, as if she was determined that someone should suffer for her plans being changed, she said:

"What are you waiting for, Anita? Surely you have the sense to realise that you should have asked Bates to bring up the tea! And hurry with your packing! You cannot wish to keep Her Grace waiting."

"No . . . no, of course not!" Anita replied.

She hurried from the room, feeling as if she had wings on her heels.

The Duke had saved her. He had really saved her! She knew that once she had escaped from Harrogate she would never return.

* * *

Driving away with the Duchess half-an-hour later, Anita found it difficult to express her gratitude in words.

"I cannot . . . begin to tell Your Grace how . . . wonderful it is of you to take me away from . . . Great-Aunt Matilda."

"I understood from my son that there was a very special reason why you should wish to leave."

"You have seen the Reverend Joshua," Anita replied. "How could I marry an . . . old man like that?"

"I think, at your age, you would naturally think any man over forty is old," the Duchess agreed.

"There is something horrible about him too," Anita said. "I do not think he is in the least worried about the natives of West Africa!"

She checked herself and looked at the Duchess apprehensively.

"I am sorry if that ... sounds ... un-Christian."

The Duchess gave a little laugh.

"I think perhaps you are prejudiced against him," she said. "And I am sure it would be easy to find you a far younger and more pleasant husband."

Anita drew in her breath.

"Please, Ma'am, I do not ... want a ... husband!" she cried in an intense little voice.

She knew the Duchess was surprised, and she explained:

"Sarah and Daphne wish to be married, but I would rather remain as I am. At least until I find ... somebody I really ... love and who ... loves me."

"I have always heard that your father and mother were very happy together," the Duchess said, "and I expect that with them as an example, that is what you are looking for in your life."

Anita looked at the Duchess in a manner she found very touching.

"At last I have found someone who understands!" she cried. "Everyone I talk to, even Sarah and His Grace, seems to think that the only thing that matters is that I should be married. I want very much more in life than just a ... wedding-ring."

The Duchess looked amused.

She did not know, as Anita's sisters did, that she had a funny way of saying things.

"And what else is it you want?" she enquired.

"Love first, of course," Anita answered seriously, "and then someone to talk intelligently to, who would understand what I was trying to say without thinking I was imagining things which did not even exist."

"I think I understand," the Duchess said. "And you will find that when you do fall in love, it is easy to talk with someone who loves you, not only with words but with your heart."

Anita gave a little cry of joy.

"You really do understand what I am saying, just

as Mama does. Oh, I am so glad that I met you! It was the luckiest thing that ever happened when I fell over your bath-chair and upset the water on your rug."

"Although I hope I can be all the things you think I am," the Duchess said, "you have to thank my son. It was he who told me I needed a Reader and suggested that I should ask your Great-Aunt to lend you to me."

"You make me sound rather as if I were a library-book!" Anita said with a smile. "But please, will you thank the Duke when you see him and tell him how very, very grateful I am?"

"You can thank him yourself, when he comes to Ollerton."

There was a little silence. Then Anita said incredulously:

"Are you saying, Your Grace, that you are taking me to Ollerton with you? That I can ... stay there?"

"That was my idea," the Duchess replied, "unless of course you wish to do something else."

"It would be a marvellous, glorious thing to do!" Anita cried. "It is only that I thought that when you had ... rescued me and taken me South you would ... want me to go ... home."

"And who is there at home?" the Duchess enquired.

After that Anita had to tell her the whole story about her mother going to Switzerland, and Sarah staying with her Aunt Elizabeth and Daphne with her Godmother.

"So there was no-one left for you," the Duchess said at the end, "but Matilda Lavenham!"

"I think she meant to be kind to me," Anita replied, "but because she admires the Reverend Joshua so much, she could never begin to understand why I do not feel the same. In fact, when she first told me he was coming to call tomorrow, I thought that he was intending to marry her."

She said this just as they reached Prospect Gardens and the Duchess was laughing as the horses came to a standstill and the footman opened the door.

*   *   *

"The Duke of Ollerton, M'Lady!" the Butler announced.

Lady Blankley, who was posed beside a huge vase of tiger-lilies, turned with affected grace towards the man standing in the doorway.

There was no mistaking her delight as she saw the Duke, looking extremely elegant, put his top-hat and stick on a chair just inside the door before he advanced towards her, a faint smile lighting his eyes.

"You are back!" she exclaimed. "I have been counting the hours, I really have! I have been so miserable without you!"

Her voice was musical in a somewhat contrived manner, but, as the Duke had often thought, everything about Lady Blankley was a polished perfection like an article fashioned by a master-craftsman.

The Duke took the hand she held out to him, kissed it, and turned it over to kiss her shell-pink palm.

Then as he straightened himself he said:

"You are even more beautiful than I remember!"

"Thank you, Kerne!"

Her eyes glittered like the emeralds she wore round her neck and he thought that her dark hair, with the blue lights in it, was very alluring.

"As I have been away for so long," the Duke said, "we have a great deal to say to each other. Shall we sit down?"

Lady Blankley moved a little closer to him.

"Why should we waste time with words?" she asked. "George is playing polo at Hurlingham and will not be back for at least another two hours."

As she spoke her arms went round the Duke's neck, pulling his head down to hers, and her lips, fiercely demanding, were on his. . . .

*   *   *

A long time later the Duke was tidying his hair in the mirror over the mantelpiece when a soft voice from the sofa asked:

"When shall I see you again?"

"I am going to Ollerton first thing tomorrow morning," the Duke replied. "I have a party arriving on Friday."

"A party?" Lady Blankley echoed. "And you have not invited me?"

The Duke shook his head.

"It is not your sort of party, Elaine, and my mother is acting as hostess."

"That would not prevent us from being together, if I were one of your guests."

The Duke told himself he had made a mistake in mentioning the fact that he was having a party, and he knew that the last person he wanted at this particular party, at which he was to choose his future wife, would be Elaine.

She was beautiful, there was no denying that. At the same time, he always left her feeling that she wanted more from him than he was willing to give.

He told himself now that although their fiery love-making was in some ways very satisfactory, he invariably had after it a feeling of disappointment which was unaccountable.

"What more do I want?" he had asked himself. "What am I looking for?"

He had thought when he first pursued Elaine Blankley, or rather she pursued him, that she was everything that any man could possibly desire.

She was beautiful, witty, and she had the polished perfection which the Duke had always sought.

She was acknowledged even by her rivals as being the best-dressed woman in London, and it was always said that when the Prince of Wales was in an irritable mood she could charm him out of it quicker than anybody else.

The Duke had found that when he made love to Elaine Blankley there was a raging, primitive fire beneath the controlled, civilised face which she showed to the world, and it inflamed him, giving them both a passionate excitement he had never known before.

And yet now the Duke told himself that there was something missing.

What it was he had no idea. He only knew that for some reason to which he could not put a name, he was glad that he was going to Ollerton tomorrow and would not be seeing Elaine again for at least ten days.

He turned from the contemplation of his reflection in the mirror to look at her.

She had a feline grace that he appreciated, and he knew that the manner in which she was lying on the sofa was deliberately provocative.

"You have made me very happy, Kerne," she said in a soft voice.

"That is what I intended to say to you, Elaine."

She held out her hand and as he took it her fingers tightened on his.

"Come again very, very soon," she said. "You know how much I miss you."

"As I shall miss you," he replied, because it was expected of him, but as he spoke he knew it was not true.

He walked to the door, picked up his hat and stick and, without saying any more, left the room.

But as he went down the broad stairs towards the Hall where a number of footmen in the Blankley livery were on duty, he asked himself whether he would ever visit this house again.

* * *

The next morning, driving his horses because the the journey to Ollerton was too short to warrant using his private train, and also because he preferred to be in the open air, the Duke of Ollerton was thinking not of Lady Blankley but of his house-party.

He had received a letter from his mother, telling him, not surprisingly, that all the people she had asked to stay had accepted her invitation.

The young girls who were coming were Lady Millicent Clyde, daughter of the Earl and Countess of Clydeshire, the Honourable Alice Down, daughter of Lord and Lady Downham, and Lady Rosemary, whom he had already met, daughter of the Marquis and Marchioness of Doncaster.

The Duchess wrote:

Having met Lady Rosemary, perhaps you have already made up your mind and the party is now unnecessary.

What was unnecessary, the Duke thought when he read his mother's letter, was that Lady Rosemary should be included in the party.

He had thought last year, although he had paid her little attention as she was still in the School-Room, that she was rather an attractive girl who might easily blossom into a beauty.

But he had been over-optimistic, and when he had arrived at the Marquis's large house which was not far from the Race-Course, he had found that Lady Rosemary was not half as interesting or as attractive as her father's horses.

There was in fact rather a horsy look about her which the Duke did not appreciate in a woman, and he thought the hearty manner in which she spoke was reminiscent of the stables where she obviously spent too much of her time.

When he rode with her and was some time in her company at the races, he realised that she was not in the least the type of woman he would invite to become his Duchess.

'Let us hope the other two are better,' he thought now as he left the outskirts of London and was in the open countryside.

Then he told himself that the whole idea of being married was so unpleasant that he had a good mind to go straight back to London to seek the familiar amusements that he found entertaining.

But he had a vision of his cousin Marmion with

his bloated red face and paunchy figure, and he knew that even if it were not his urgent desire to prevent him from succeeding to the Dukedom, he still had to obey what was to all intents and purposes a command from the Queen.

Yet, every instinct in his body rebelled against it.

He had no wish to be married and he knew only too well that even if he had some sort of interest or even an ordinary natural desire for his wife as a woman, it would very quickly fade.

Elaine Blankley was a case in point.

He had known when he went to bed last night that he was through with her, and although she would doubtless protest and perhaps make a scene if she could get him alone, her name was crossed off his list, and that excluded her from being a guest at Ollerton.

"I wonder who will interest me next," the Duke asked himself, and he thought that the inevitable end of a chase which never took very long was becoming tedious.

"Why are all women so exactly alike?" he asked.

When he met a new beauty for the first time he found himself intrigued like a man exploring new territory or finding a strange, hitherto uncatalogued flower on the side of a mountain.

Then all too quickly he found he knew every move of the game before she made it.

It was like playing chess with an opponent who was so bad that there was never a chance of it being anything but a walkover.

Sometimes he would think that a woman was mysterious and elusive, only to find quite soon that there was nothing Sphinx-like about her and all she wanted was to be in his arms as quickly as possible.

"Dammit all," the Duke said to himself, "I think I shall go big-game shooting."

Then he knew he had done that already, and, what was more, his future was waiting for him at Ollerton—three fair-haired, blue-eyed young women who were tall enough to look resplendent in the

Ollerton tiaras, with Junoesque figures to do credit to the ropes of Ollerton pearls.

* * *

The Duchess had said very much the same thing to Anita when they were travelling down in the train from Harrogate.

Anita had been thrilled and excited by the Duke's train as a child might have been.

"I thought only the Queen had a private train," she had said, "but of course a Duke is very nearly the same as King, is he not?"

"Not exactly!" the Duchess had said, smiling, "although I am sure Kerne would like to think he was."

"He looks so magnificent and it is only right that he should have everything to enhance his position," Anita said ingenuously. "I am sure when he was a little boy he had a toy train and planned that when he was grown up he would have a real one."

"That certainly never struck me," the Duchess said, "but we will ask him sometime if that was true."

She smiled at Anita, who sat first on one seat of the Drawing-Room compartment, then on another, determined to try out everything.

As servants wearing the Duke's livery brought them luncheon, her eyes were shining and the Duchess thought she looked as if she were watching her first Pantomime.

"I ought to have read to you," Anita said when they had been travelling for a long time and the Duchess said she would go to her sleeping-compartment to lie down.

"I have enjoyed our conversation, dear," the Duchess replied, "and actually I do not really require a Reader."

She saw the disappointment in Anita's eyes and guessed she was thinking that in that case she would dispense with her services very quickly.

"At the same time, I like having you with me,"

she said, "and because my private secretary is away on holiday, you shall help me, when we get to Ollerton, to arrange the special party that my son is giving."

"A special party?" Anita questioned.

"Yes," the Duchess answered, "and that is why you and I are going to stay in the big house and not in the Dower House where I live when I am alone."

"Tell me, please, tell me exactly what you do!" Anita begged.

She listened with rapt attention while the Duchess explained how sometimes the Duke had parties at Ollerton at which he wanted his mother to be the Chaperone, but otherwise she lived in her own house, which was smaller and very beautiful and where she had all her special things round her.

"Which do you like the best?" Anita asked.

"It is difficult to say," the Duchess replied. "When I first left Ollerton, where I had lived all the years since I became a bride, I am afraid I shed a few tears as I felt I was saying good-bye to my youth. Then I came to love my own house, and it is rather nice to be able to do exactly what I want without worrying too much about appearances."

"I can understand that," Anita said. "But now we are to go to Ollerton?"

"Yes, because this party is a very special one."

"Why is it so special?" Anita enquired.

The Duchess told her the truth.

She was almost certain that Anita was not having romantic dreams about the Duke, but one could never be sure with young girls, and the Duchess wished not only to save her son from any embarrassment but to prevent this engaging child from having her heart broken.

She began to tell Anita exactly what the Duke required of his wife, and she thought, from the manner in which she listened and the enthusiasm with which she asked questions, that she had been quite needlessly apprehensive in thinking that Anita had any foolish aspirations in his direction.

"You must find him somebody very, very beautiful," Anita said.

"That is what I am trying to do," the Duchess answered. "But it is not easy. You see, my son is used to associating with much older women who are sophisticated, witty, elegant, and amusing. This is something impossible to find in a girl who is just out of the School-Room."

Anita nodded her head.

"I can understand that," she said, "and I expect most of them find it very frightening to be launched into the world like a ship which has never been in the water before."

"That is true," the Duchess smiled, "and sometimes it seems like a rough sea."

Anita laughed.

"No-one ever looks her best when she is seasick!"

"I am trying," the Duchess continued, "to find three girls from whom my son will be able to choose a wife who will fulfil all his requirements."

"You will be able to help her," Anita said, "but she will find it difficult, Your Grace, to be as charming or as beautiful as you!"

The Duchess thought she was almost echoing what the Duke had said, and she smiled before she answered:

"It is very sweet of you to speak like that, but I am growing old, and I know that my tiresome rheumatism has put lines on my face, besides making me walk in a grotesque fashion."

Anita thought for a moment. Then she said:

"Would Your Grace think it very impertinent of me if I made a suggestion?"

"Of course not," the Duchess replied.

"Well, we had a Doctor in Fenchurch who was rather a friend of Papa and Mama, and he treated people in the village suffering from rheumatism and he always made them better."

"How did he do that?"

"First, he insisted that they should always walk quite a long distance every day. He said it was fatal for them to become chair-bound because sooner or later they became bed-bound, and then there was no hope for them."

The Duchess looked at Anita in a startled fashion.

"I never thought of that," she said. "I wonder if you are right!"

"I am sure Dr. Emerson was right," Anita said, "and also he used to give his patients a herbal drink which he sometimes asked Mama to make for him, and I can make some for you, if you wish."

"I would try anything to take away the pain and make me mobile again," the Duchess replied.

Anita was silent for a moment. Then she said:

"That day at the well when I fell over your chair, I was thinking how wonderful it would be if the water really worked for those who drank it and they all jumped out of their bath-chairs and shouted that they were cured."

She paused before adding:

"I said a little prayer that that might happen, but instead I met you and it was the most wonderful thing that ever happened to me! Perhaps if you drink the herbs and I pray very hard while I am mixing them, they may work like a miracle and you will be well, completely well, and your rheumatism will go away."

"That is a lovely idea," the Duchess said, "and of course we will try it. I too believe prayer can do amazing and unexpected things."

"Mama always said that God helps those who help themselves," Anita replied, "so we must do our part too."

"That is exactly what we will do," the Duchess agreed.

When they left the train at the Halt which was used only by visitors to Ollerton Park, Anita saw there was waiting an open carriage with a white piqué awning to shade them from the sun.

They drove for a little way through pretty country, wooded and with meadowland billiant with wild flowers.

Then suddenly ahead of them was Ollerton Park and it was even more magnificent and impressive than Anita had expected.

"It is beautiful, magnificent!" she cried. "It is exactly the sort of house the Duke should have! Do you not feel that too, Your Grace?"

"I do indeed," the Duchess replied. "And I felt just like you do the first time I came here after I was engaged."

"You must have felt that you were stepping into fairy-land," Anita said, "and I am sure you looked exactly like the Princess who married Prince Charming."

The Duchess smiled.

She was beginning to realise that everything Anita said or thought had a dream-like quality that had little to do with reality.

She thought it was very unusual to find a girl who was so completely unselfconscious and had about her a vivid joy in life which made her different from any young woman the Duchess had ever met before.

Because she had only just thought of it, she said:

"Yes, Ollerton is a fairy-tale building, and I think, Anita, because I hope you will stay with me for some time, that I should give you some gowns which will be complementary to the house in which you will be staying."

Anita turned to look at her and the Duchess thought that her blue eyes were shining like stars.

"New gowns!" she cried. "Oh, Ma'am, do you mean it? If you do, it will be the most wonderful, exciting thing that could possibly happen."

She paused. Then before the Duchess could speak she said quickly:

"I am sure I should not ... accept such a generous present from you when you have been so kind

68

already in helping me ... escape from the ... Reverend Joshua."

"There are a great many more exciting things to do," the Duchess said quietly, "and I do mean that you shall have some new gowns. You will enjoy Ollerton all the more if you feel you are dressed for the part."

"But of course," Anita said, "and please ... do you think I could have a new crinoline ... a really big one?"

She saw the smile on the Duchess's face and added quickly:

"Perhaps not an enormous one ... because I should look strange as I am so small ... but just one that is fashionable."

"I will get you one that is exactly right," the Duchess promised.

Anita clasped her hands together.

"I am dreaming ... I know I am dreaming!" she said. "But I do hope I shall not wake up until I have worn it!"

Once again the Duchess was laughing as the horses came to a standstill.

Chapter Four

The Duke walked up the steps and into the magnificent marble Hall.

The statues were all of goddesses, and he thought, as he had often thought before, that there was no Hall to rival his in any other of the large houses he had visited.

"Welcome back, Your Grace," the Butler said respectfully. "Her Grace is in the Music-Room."

The Duke handed the Butler his hat and gloves, and was feeling satisfied that the six footmen in the Ollerton livery were up to standard.

He had always insisted that they must be over six feet tall and their smartness and bearing was something on which he was particularly insistent.

Leaving the Hall, he walked down a wide corridor hung with portraits of his ancestors which led to the Music-Room, which was in the West Wing.

It was a room that had been redecorated by the Duchess shortly before his father's death and it was in consequence artistic and combined the classical and the modern with great success.

As the Duke drew nearer to it, he expected to hear the music of Chopin or Bach, knowing that they were his mother's favourite Composers.

To his surprise, he heard the unexpected sound of a gay waltz which had been popular in London the previous winter and to which he had partnered many fascinating beauties.

70

Now that he thought of it, he remembered that it was during this waltz at a Ball given at Marlborough House that he had first been aware of Elaine Blankley's attractions.

She had used every known artifice to make him aware of her as a woman, glancing up at him with her green eyes veiled by her mascaraed eye-lashes and making her hand on his shoulder feel like a caress.

That he should recall Elaine at this moment when he had returned home annoyed him, and there was a slight frown between the Duke's eyes as he opened the door into the Music-Room.

Then he stood still in utter astonishment.

In the centre of the room was his mother and he could hardly believe his eyes when he saw that she was dancing.

She was moving slowly, it was true, but very gracefully, and from the manner in which she held her arms there was no doubt that she was pretending to be waltzing with a partner to a melody played on the huge Broadwood piano at which Anita was sitting.

As the Duchess turned she saw her son and came to a standstill, then a second or two later Anita realised who had come into the room and raised her hands from the key-board.

The Duke spoke and there was no mistaking the amazement in his voice.

"You are dancing, Mama! How is it possible?"

The Duchess would have replied, but before she could do so Anita came running to her across the floor to exclaim:

"You have done it! You have done it! Is it not wonderful? And you told me you would never dance again!"

"But, as you see, I can waltz," the Duchess said.

"Is this what Harrogate has done for you?" the Duke asked.

The Duchess shook her head.

71

"It helped a little, but that I have been walking and can dance is due entirely to Anita."

"To Anita?" the Duke echoed.

As he spoke he looked at the small figure standing beside him, but her eyes, filled with delight, were on the Duchess's face.

"Anita made me walk and gave me a herbal concoction to drink which I really do believe has performed miracles!"

"It certainly has!" the Duke agreed. "I never expected to see you dance again, Mama, nor for that matter to walk so easily."

"But now I can do both," the Duchess said, "and it is due entirely to this dear child."

She put out her hand to Anita as she spoke.

"You must not forget one important thing, Ma'am," Anita said, "that we both prayed very hard for a miracle."

"Yes, of course," the Duchess agreed. "That is something we must not forget."

Anita looked at the Duke.

"I was praying for a miracle," she said. "when I fell over Her Grace's bath-chair in the Pump Room at Harrogate."

"But instead you 'fell from grace,'" the Duke said with a smile.

"No," Anita replied, "it was the miracle I was asking for, but it came in a most mysterious manner."

She gave a little skip of joy as she went on:

"It was a miracle that you saved me from having to marry the Reverend Joshua; a miracle that brought me here; and a very, very big miracle that the herbs and our prayers have made your mother so much better that she can dance!"

The Duke smiled.

"Do you agree with that, Mama?"

"But of course!" the Duchess answered. "But now, miracle or no miracle, I would like to sit down for a moment."

The Duke led her to a comfortable sofa and as the Duchess sat down on it Anita said, with a note of anxiety in her voice:

"It has not all been too much for you? Shall I call the footmen to bring your chair so that you can be carried upstairs to lie down?"

"No, I am perfectly all right," the Duchess replied. "It is just that I need a moment to 'catch my breath,' so that I can talk to my son."

"Then I will leave you to talk to His Grace," Anita said tactfully.

"I think first you should show him your new gown," the Duchess suggested.

The Duke looked at Anita and realised why she seemed different.

Now, instead of the plain little dress he had seen on her in Harrogate with its white collar and cuffs, she was wearing an extremely attractive and obviously expensive white gown with a wide skirt that was unmistakably supported by a crinoline.

Above it her tiny waist was encircled by a blue sash, and her pale hair was dressed in a new fashion which made her look, he thought, even more like a small angel than she had before.

After what she had accomplished for his mother, he almost expected to see wings sprouting from her shoulders, especially when she twirled round to show him her gown from the back, saying:

"Her Grace has been so kind, and I never, never in my whole life expected to have such lovely gowns as she has given me. They are definitely part of my miracle."

"And a very becoming one," the Duke said.

There was a slightly mocking note in his voice and Anita was not certain whether he was pleased or thought it presumptuous of her to accept such expensive presents from his mother.

"I want to talk with you, Kerne," the Duchess said, "but before we do so, I would like you to see the way Anita and I have arranged the Ball-Room."

73

The Duke raised his eye-brows.

"The Ball-Room?"

"Yes, dearest, we are giving a Ball on Saturday night. I thought it would make the party go with a swing and melt away any embarrassment there might be among our younger guests."

She thought there was a slightly ominous look in her son's eyes, and she added quickly:

"It will only be a very small Ball, just the house-party and our friends in the immediate neighbour-hood. I do hope the idea pleases you."

"Of course, I am delighted with whatever arrangements you have made," the Duke said hastily.

"Then go and look at the Ball-Room," the Duchess suggested, "and if it is not to your liking, then of course we can—change things."

The way his mother spoke told the Duke that it would be a difficult thing to do.

Because he wished to please her, he rose to his feet and Anita ran ahead of him towards the door.

Only as they walked together down the passage which led to the Ball-Room in another part of the great house did she say, a little nervously:

"I do hope you do not ... mind my ... staying here as your mother ... asked me to do. She has also ... invited me to be ... present at your ... Ball."

There was no mistaking the anxiety in her voice, as if she was afraid he might disapprove, but the Duke replied:

"As you are so small, I daresay we can squeeze you in!"

She knew he was teasing her, and once again she gave a little skip as she walked beside him and said:

"It is so very, very exciting! I have never been to a Ball before, and my gown is so beautiful!"

She paused, then she said in a different tone:

"I have been waiting ever since I came to Ollerton for you to arrive so that I could thank you. I have never been so happy as I am here with your mother.

We have had such fun arranging the Ball-Room, which I hope will be to your liking."

It struck the Duke that most girls of Anita's age might have found it rather dull even at Ollerton to be alone with an older woman and with no other distractions for nearly two weeks.

But there was no doubt that Anita's eyes were shining and there was an excitement as well as a sincerity in what she said which made it impossible not to believe that she spoke the truth.

They reached the Ball-Room and the Duke standing in the doorway stared about him in surprise.

He had always thought that the long Ball-Room, which had been added at the beginning of Queen Victoria's reign, was not a particularly interesting addition to the house, which was otherwise a fine example of Adam architecture.

Now it was transformed and he wondered how much the transformation owed to Anita's imagination.

Instead of the cream-coloured walls with somewhat pretentious pillars and uninspired decorations, the whole room had been converted into a picture of Venice.

At the far end there was a mural which made him think he was looking onto the canal by moonlight with San Marco in the distance. In the foreground there were lighted gondolas being propelled along the smooth water.

From the ceiling were hung curtains of crimson satin which made the room appear like a tent, and it was lit by the traditional gold lanterns of Venice.

Round the floor in place of the conventional chairs were benches covered with silk cushions and with a high prow at one end such as was to be found on every gondola.

The Duke was aware that Anita was watching his face with a worried expression in her eyes, and after a pause he said:

"Very effective, and something we have not seen at Ollerton before!"

"You really like it?"

"I can certainly recognise it for the place it is supposed to be," the Duke replied.

Anita gave a little cry of delight.

"That is what I hoped you would say. Her Grace has never visited Venice, so we had to rely on the pictures we could find in books in the Library."

"I have a feeling," the Duke said, "this was your idea and you tempted my mother into such extravagance."

"Her Grace did say she thought the room was rather ugly and that perhaps if we had garlands of flowers or something like that, it would be an improvement."

"But instead, prompted by one of your daydreams, you thought up this idea of Venice."

"You are pleased . . . you really are . . . pleased?" Anita asked anxiously.

"I think you would be very disappointed if I said anything different," the Duke replied.

"I wanted you not to see it until Saturday night," Anita said, "but Her Grace was just a little afraid that you would think it too fanciful."

"I cannot imagine our guests will be able to say such complimentary things as an Italian gallant would manage to do," the Duke said, "but at least I hope they do their best to produce the right amount of romance that you are expecting."

Again he was teasing Anita, and he saw a little flush come into her face and knew without her saying so that because of her experience at Harrogate, she would resist the idea of any man approaching her amorously.

It was an attitude he had not expected.

At the same time, he thought it was inevitable, after she had been so frightened by the idea of being forced to marry her Great-Aunt's pet Parson, that she would be afraid of all men.

'She is very young,' he thought to himself, 'and of course, to her, being brought up in a small village, men are an unknown quantity. It would be a pity if she avoids them too strenuously and misses a lot of fun.'

Then he thought that if in fact she did begin to enjoy being pursued by men, the compliments they would pay her and the flirtations they would expect, it would undoubtedly spoil the child-like atmosphere she created which made her resemble a small angel.

He saw now that she had moved nearer to the mural at the end of the room and was staring at the gondolas on the canal as if she could really see them and the exquisite piazzas behind them.

"Are you praying that one day a miracle will carry you to the most glamorous city in the world?" the Duke asked.

"I was thinking of its history," Anita replied. "When I was looking for pictures of it, I read how the Venetians wasted their lives in pleasure-seeking and so lost their power and even their trade. It seems such a pity."

"Are you really saying that pleasure-seeking is a waste of time?" the Duke enquired.

"I think everyone wants pleasure," Anita replied seriously. "At the same time, it should be earned, like a holiday."

The Duke did not speak, and after a moment she said:

"Your mother has told me how regularly you speak in the House of Lords and how you work at bringing your houses and your Estate to perfection. That is why I so wanted this party to be an enjoyable one for you, especially as there is a particular reason for its being given."

The Duke frowned again.

If there was one thing he disliked, it was having his private affairs talked about, even by his mother.

Then somehow, because Anita had spoken so

naturally, it did not annoy him as much as it might have done had she been somebody else.

As if she knew that she had spoken too seriously, she said lightly:

"The scene is set, everything is ready, and it only remains for you to play the part of Paris."

There was a lilt in her voice, as if she found the idea extremely romantic, and the Duke with a wry twist of his lips replied:

"So you are suggesting it is the Golden Apple I am to present?"

Anita gave a little chuckle.

"I think, Your Grace, it is really a coronet, but I expect whoever receives it will feel it is one and the same thing!"

The Duke thought this was really going too far and he felt that it was a definite impertinence.

Then, before he could remonstrate with her, she said:

"I must not stay here talking. Her Grace will be longing to know what you feel about the room. She was so afraid it might not please you. But I will tell her that everything is all right."

She spoke the last words over her shoulder as she began to run along the dance-floor, and before the Duke could think of anything to say, she had disappeared through the door by which they had entered the room.

It was certainly unusual, he thought, for a woman, when she could be alone with him, to hurry away to talk to somebody else!

As he walked slowly back to the front of the house he thought he had been extremely clever to rescue Anita from a disastrous marriage and at the same time to find somebody to amuse and help his mother.

At dinner that evening there were only the three of them and the Duke put himself out to entertain not only the Duchess but Anita, who looked at him with wide eyes and listened with rapt attention to everything he had to say.

At the same time, she was not in the least shy and she made occasional quaint little remarks which made him laugh.

Because he realised that it was no use standing on his dignity when Anita obviously had the full confidence of his mother, they talked quite naturally and without reserve about the three girls who had been invited to Ollerton to meet him.

"I do not mind telling you, Mama," the Duke said, "that Rosemary Castor, on second acquaintance, was extremely disappointing."

"I am sorry to hear that," the Duchess said. "I thought you said last year that she seemed an attractive young woman."

"She is now over-hearty, and she gave me the impression of looking like a well-bred horse!" the Duke remarked.

The Duchess smiled a little ruefully and Anita said:

"When I went down to your stables and saw your horses, I knew I would much rather marry one of them than the Reverend Joshua."

"I was just wondering," the Duke replied teasingly, "if your pedigree is good enough for you to be a suitable bride for Thunderer or Hercules!"

Anita knew he was referring to his two finest stallions, which she had already been told were the pride of his stable.

"I certainly would not aspire as high as either!" she flashed. "But yesterday Thunderer did allow me, with great condescension, to pat his neck and hand him a carrot!"

The Duke frowned.

"You must be careful," he said. "Thunderer is not always to be trusted. I hope you did not go into his stall?"

"I am not answering that question," Anita replied,

"in case you are angry with me or your Head-Groom!"

"I suppose you are trying to tell me that through some Divine protection even my horses will not hurt you."

"If I say 'yes' it will sound conceited," Anita replied. "If I say 'no' it might be unlucky!"

The Duke laughed.

"You are not the angel you pretend to be," he said. "I think that in fact you are so devious in your ways, Anita, that you belong to another hemisphere altogether."

"If you recognise me," Anita answered quickly, "there is nothing I can say to defend myself!"

The Duke was amused by the sharpness of her mind and they sparred and argued with each other until the meal ended.

He rather expected, because it would be the usual procedure among his guests, that when his mother retired to bed immediately after dinner, Anita would make some excuse to continue their conversation and remain with him.

Instead she went upstairs with the Duchess and he did not see her again that night.

The following morning after breakfast he went to the stables as he usually did, to look at his horses, and found that Anita was already there.

She was in fact standing inside Thunderer's stall giving him a carrot with one hand and patting his neck with the other.

The Duke watched her for some minutes before she was aware of his presence. Then she looked round and saw him, and there was a faint flush on her cheeks as she said:

"Your Grace is early! I understood that you did not come to the stables before nine-thirty."

"So you were stealing a march on me!"

"I thought I should not come today, as you are here," Anita replied, "but then I thought that Thunderer might miss the carrot I always give him."

"Then I presume, having ingratiated yourself with my horses," the Duke commented, "that you will expect me to take you riding."

He saw by the expression in Anita's eyes that she had never thought such a thing.

She looked into his face to see if he was serious before she said:

"Would you ... do you mean that? Could I ... go with you? I have ridden once since I have been here, but I did not like to leave Her Grace alone."

"What is my mother doing at the moment?" the Duke enquired.

"She is having her hair washed," Anita answered, "so that she will look beautiful, as she always does, when your guests arrive this afternoon."

"In which case I presume you are off-duty?"

He paused, knowing that Anita was tense as she waited, almost like one of his dogs who sensed he was about to be taken for a walk.

The Duke drew his watch from his waist-coat pocket and said:

"I will give you exactly five minutes in which to change. I will wait for you at the front door, and if you are any longer I shall leave without you!"

Anita gave a cry of delight.

Then she was running from the stables, holding up her crinoline with both hands as she did so.

The Duke watched her go, then began to talk to his Head-Groom about the horses he had not seen for some weeks.

*　　*　　*

A little later, riding across the Park, he thought Anita, on a horse that seemed too big for her, looked extremely attractive in a tight-waisted habit of blue piqué and a high hat trimmed with a gauze veil.

The Duke had chosen too many gowns for a succession of lovely ladies over the years not to be a connoisseur of a woman's appearance, and he was aware that his mother, with unerring good taste, had chosen for Anita clothes that were perfect for both her height and her youth.

But no dressmaker could improve her flower-like face, the shining innocence and excitement in her blue eyes, or the mischievous little smile which often twisted her cupid's-bow mouth.

She was certainly an engaging little creature, the Duke thought to himself, and knew he had been right in thinking that she had a way with horses which was something which could not be taught.

Riding beside him, Anita knew that no man could look more handsome, appearing to be an indivisible part of the horse on which he was mounted.

Her imagination made her wonder if in fact there were any animals to be found in Hades.

Then she told herself that animals were born without sin, and if they became bad-tempered or savage it was due entirely to the treatment they received from mankind.

No, Heaven would be filled with animals, for it would not be Heaven without them, while in Hell it would be one of the things one longed for and could not have.

The Duke's voice broke in on her thoughts:

"What are you thinking about?"

Because she did not wish to say that indirectly she was thinking of him, she replied:

"I was thinking of animals and of how much they mean in our lives."

"Have you owned many?" he enquired.

"Papa had a number of horses until his accident, and of course we had dogs, and when I was small I had a cat who used to sleep curled up on my bed."

"And that taught you how to handle a horse like Thunderer?"

"I think the answer to that is that I love him and he knows it," Anita answered. "It is much easier for a horse, and I suppose any animal, to be aware of what we are thinking and feeling than it is for us nowadays to feel the same about a human being."

"Why 'nowadays'?" the Duke asked curiously.

"Because we do not use our sixth sense."

"Do you think that is what you were doing when you recognised me the first time we met?"

"No," Anita replied, "I was seeing with my eyes. It was not until later, when you were so kind to me and helped me to escape, that I realised you had not fallen from Heaven as I imagined but in fact were living in it here at Ollerton."

"I wish that were true."

"But it is true!" Anita said positively. "How can you be so ungrateful?"

"Ungrateful?"

"Not to recognise that there is no place which could be more beautiful or more perfect than the house and Estate that belong to you. Besides which, you have a mother who loves you more than anyone else in the world."

Anita's voice was soft as she spoke of the Duchess.

For a little while they rode on in silence, and it was inevitable that the Duke's mind was on the young women who were arriving to stay that afternoon; one of whom, as his wife, would share with him the perfection of Ollerton.

Strangely, as if she could read his thoughts without his saying them aloud, Anita asked very quietly:

"Must you do this?"

It did not strike the Duke that he should resent her familiarity with his private affairs. Instead he replied:

"I have no alternative. If this party is a failure, there must be another, and yet another. But the end will be the same. I cannot escape!"

Almost as if he could not bear to think of it, he touched Thunderer with his whip and the stallion responded by breaking into a gallop, and there was no chance of continuing the conversation.

Only when they reached home and Anita went up to her bedroom to change did she stand at the window looking out over the Park in which she had just been riding.

The sunshine was glinting on the huge oak trees and on the lake, on which white swans moved with exquisite grace.

"Please, God, let him find someone who will make him happy," she prayed in her heart.

Then quickly, because she thought the Duchess would be waiting for her, she began to change into one of her beautiful new gowns.

As she expected, because they had travelled in the Duke's train and had driven in his comfortable carriages from the Halt, the majority of the party arrived exactly on time.

The Duchess was waiting for them in the Silver Salon, which was on the ground floor, and Anita had put on one of her prettiest gowns.

"Do you want me to be there, Ma'am?" she asked. "Perhaps you and His Grace would prefer to receive your guests alone?"

"No, of course not, dear child," the Duchess replied, "and I think you will be a great help, since this house-party is very unlike Kerne's usual ones."

"You mean because the girls you have invited are so young?"

"Exactly!" the Duchess agreed.

"There is no reason why they should be difficult to talk to, or not enjoy themselves," Anita said. "I am sure Sarah is the life and soul of every party she goes to in London. Mama used to say that Sarah always made a party go."

"I hope you will do the same," the Duchess said with a smile.

Anita knew that Her Grace was apprehensive but she could not understand why.

The Marquis and Marchioness of Doncaster came into the Salon first and the Duke was obviously delighted to see them.

Their daughter, Lady Rosemary, was presented

to the Duchess, and immediately Anita knew why she
was not in the least suitable to be the wife of the
Duke.

There was something "horsy" about her, there
was no grace in the way she walked, and she shook
hands almost as a man might have done.

The Earl and Countess of Clydeshire's daughter
was, however, very different.

She was tall, golden-haired and blue-eyed, and
was in fact, Anita thought, extremely pretty.

She had a quiet, rather repressed manner of
talking, but that, Anita guessed, was because she was
shy.

She moved to her side to ask her if she had had a
good journey.

"It was the first time I have been in a private
train, and I thought it very luxurious," Lady Millicent
answered.

"I thought it was fascinating," Anita said, "and I
could hardly believe it was real."

"It was real enough to me!" Lady Millicent replied in a voice Anita did not understand.

There were other friends of the Duke's who had
been on the train, one a married couple who were
extremely keen on racing, and the other a slightly
older man called Lord Greshame.

"Glad to be here, Ollerton!" he said now to the
Duke. "I have always said that you have the best
horses and the most comfortable houses in the whole
country."

"That is exactly the sort of compliment I like to
receive, George," the Duke replied. "I think you know
everybody except Miss Lavenham."

Lord Greshame shook hands with Anita, but before he could speak to her, Lord and Lady Downham
and their daughter Alice were announced.

They had driven down from London and had
managed, as Lord Downham averred in a loud voice,
to beat his previous record by ten minutes fifty sec-
onds.

Lady Alice was, Anita thought, looking at her, a disappointment.

She was of course tall, fair, and blue-eyed, but she had a somewhat sulky expression, was too fat to be attractive, and there were undoubtedly spots on her chin.

'Lady Millicent will certainly have it all her own way!' Anita thought, and wondered what the Duchess would think of her prospective daughter-in-law.

There were a number of other guests who arrived in the next hour, making the number staying in the house up to twenty.

"You must be very busy downstairs," Anita said to the maid who looked after her when she was getting her bath ready.

"Not as busy as we are sometimes, Miss," the maid replied. "His Grace has had as many as forty guests staying in the house, and that means, as most of them brings a lady's-maid or a valet, nearly forty extra in the Servants' Hall and Housekeeper's room."

"Then it is a party for you too," Anita said with a smile.

"That's what I feels, Miss," the maid said, "although the older ones grumble."

"I expect they enjoy it really."

She remembered how Deborah often grumbled when there were extra people to meals at home.

But during the time when there had been very few visitors she had complained because, she said, there was no life about the place.

'There is certainly plenty of life at Ollerton!' Anita thought.

When she was ready and looked at herself in the mirror she could hardly believe that the attractive, fashionable reflection she saw was really that of Anita Lavenham.

She had written long letters to both her sisters to tell them what was happening to her, and Sarah had replied saying how delighted she was and how she had to make the very best of her opportunity of meeting important people at Ollerton.

She had written:

> *Perhaps, dearest, one of the Duke's friends may take a fancy to you, and if he does, please be practical. You may never have such an opportunity again! Although I agree that it was ridiculous of Great-Aunt Matilda to expect you to marry an aged Parson, I am sure you will realise that the alternative, when the Duchess is tired of you, is to go back to Fenchurch and become an Old Maid.*
>
> *I am saying nothing yet, because it might be unlucky, but I am keeping my fingers crossed that I might, I just might, have very special news for you in a few weeks. Oh, Anita, please pray that what I am wishing for will come true, because it is what I want more than I have ever wanted anything before.*

'Sarah is in love,' Anita thought as she read the letter, and because she loved her sister she prayed very hard that Sarah might have her wish.

Later that evening, when they were all sitting talking in the Drawing-Room, which was one of the most beautiful rooms in the house, at the Duchess's suggeston Anita moved to the piano.

The Duchess had already told her when they had been talking about the party that she thought music always made people relax and took away some of the stiffness between those who had just met one another for the first time.

Anita therefore chose soft, rather romantic music, knowing that in fact she played it better than the more classical studies which were really Her Grace's favourites.

"Mama taught me to play," she had told the Duchess. "She was really good. I only strum to amuse myself."

"I think you play very prettily," the Duchess said.
"It is a talent more women should have, and a very
attractive one."

Anita therefore played what she thought would
make a happy background for the Duke's guests, but
her thoughts swept away towards her own family.

"Please, God, help Sarah find a husband," she
prayed in her heart, "and let Daphne find one too, but
prevent me from having to be in a hurry to choose
anyone."

She was praying so intensely that her eyes were
closed, and she started as she heard the Duke say:

"What are you thinking about in the darkness of
your mind?"

She opened her eyes to find that he was leaning
on the piano, looking at her.

"I . . . was thinking."

"About whom?"

"My sister Sarah."

"I heard when I was in London that she was a
great success. In fact, I forgot to tell you, I actually
saw her at one party I attended."

"Did you think she looked pretty?"

"Very, but you are not in the least like her."

"I know," Anita admitted. "Sarah is the beauty
of the family."

Her eyes lit up as she added:

"If you have heard she is a success, perhaps what
she is wishing for has come true. Actually, I was
praying that it would."

"For what is she wishing?"

"I think, although she has not exactly said so, that
she is in love," Anita confided.

"Then let us hope she catches the man on whom
she has set her heart," the Duke remarked.

Anita felt that the way he had said this grated on
her, but she knew it was impossible to find fault with
him.

Sarah was in fact trying to catch a husband and
Daphne was doing the same thing.

'It is something I will never . . . never . . . do!' Anita silently swore to herself.

Then she realised that the Duke was still looking at her, and although it seemed impossible and she could not explain how, she felt that he knew exactly what she was thinking.

"Later you will change your mind," he said, almost as if she had spoken aloud. "Then you will be like every woman, chasing some wretched man when nature intended that he should chase you."

The way he spoke was so harsh, so unpleasant, that Anita stared at him wide-eyed and the music died beneath her figners.

Then before she could reply, before she could even deny the charge he had levelled at her, he walked back to his guests.

Chapter Five

The Duke, having performed four duty-dances with the most distinguished of his guests, thought the moment had come when he must dance with the girls who had been invited for his inspection.

He had already decided, as Anita had done, that the only one who was even possibly acceptable was Lady Millicent Clyde.

Although her father, the Earl, was somewhat of a bore in the House of Lords, he certainly appreciated good horse-flesh and his house in Huntingdonshire was extremely comfortable.

The Duke had realised the moment the Ball started that his mother—or perhaps, if he was fair, Anita—had been right in decorating the Ball-Room and making it, if nothing else, a good talking-point.

The guests who had come from the County were both surprised and delighted by the decorative effect of Venice, and the Orchestra which had come down from London provided exactly the right type of music.

This was sometimes soft and romantic and at other times gay and spirited, and even if the Duke had wished to find fault, he would have found it impossible not to be aware that the party was going with "a swing."

He knew too that it was a delight he had not expected that his mother was so well and had actually danced with the Lord Lieutenant.

She was looking exceedingly beautiful and was wearing a satin gown of dove-grey, which had been made fashionable by Princess Alexandra, against which the unique Ollerton sapphires looked magnificent.

The Duke thought, as he had so many times before, that it would be impossible for him to find a wife who looked as lovely as his mother or had a character like hers.

He was well aware that the compliments she was paid by everybody present came not only because they admired her but because they loved her.

She had been instrumental in so many reforms that were vitally needed in the County, and she had never been too busy to listen to the troubles of other people whether they were high or low in rank.

It seemed to the Duke as if his father's words kept echoing incessantly in his ears when he had said: "They do not make women like that these days!"

However, duty was duty, and as he walked across the room to where Lady Millicent was standing beside her mother, the Countess, he knew exactly where his duty lay.

Lady Millicent was in fact looking very attractive.

Anita had thought so when they had all congregated before dinner in the Silver Salon.

Her gown of white lace billowing out from a small waist was in a fashion which had been set by the Empress Eugénie and which was particularly becoming for young girls.

Her eyes were blue and her hair was exactly the right burnished gold that the Duke had insisted he required in his wife.

"May I have the pleasure of this dance?" he asked.

As he spoke he expected Lady Millicent's blue eyes to light up with the glint of excitement which he had always seen in any woman's eyes when he invited her to partner him on the dance-floor.

91

But Lady Millicent merely inclined her head, and it was the Countess who said eagerly:

"That would be delightful, my dear Duke, and you will find that Milly is a very good dancer."

"I am sure I shall," the Duke replied briefly.

Then as the Orchestra began to play a waltz by Offenbach, he led her onto the dance-floor.

As he did so, he was aware that she was also the right height that he had stipulated as being important in someone who would do justice to the Ollerton diamonds and the five strings of Oriental pearls which had once belonged to a Maharajah of India.

One of the Duke's ancestors, who had been one of the first Governor-Generals, had bought them for what now seemed a "song," and every subsequent Duchess had found them extremely becoming.

"Pearls must be worn against the skin," they had been told, and they had not needed this encouragement to drape themselves in what had often been valued at "a king's ransom."

"I hope you are enjoying yourself at Ollerton, Lady Millicent," the Duke said as they moved sedately over the polished floor.

"Yes, thank you."

Her reply was conventional and her voice undoubtedly flat.

"I am sure you find the decorations of the Ball-Room unusual, and I must admit they surprised me when I first saw them."

"It looks very pretty!"

"You have never been to Venice?"

"No."

The Duke thought with a rising feeling of irritation that this was hard going.

Persevering, he said:

"It is a city I find very beautiful, and of course, as I expect you have been told, it is the perfect place for honeymooners."

To his surprise, Lady Millicent stiffened and missed a step. Then she said:

"I believe the canals make it very unhealthy."

"I think it depends in what part of Venice you stay," the Duke replied. "Near the lagoon you have the advantage of the tides."

"All the same, I would not like to visit Venice."

He decided, from the way in which Lady Millicent spoke, that this was definitely the end of that subject, and he told himself that if she had no wish to talk he was quite prepared to remain silent.

Then across the room he saw his mother watching him and knew he must make a further effort.

"Your father has some excellent horses," he said. "Are you fond of riding?"

"Not particularly."

"Then what do you enjoy?"

There was a definite hesitation before Lady Millicent replied:

"Quite a—number of things."

The Duke knew that if they had actually been married at this moment he would have wanted to shake her. Instead, he said with an undoubtedly cynical note in his voice:

"That is certainly very enlightening!"

"I cannot think why you should be—interested."

The words came almost inaudibly, and yet he heard them, and he told himself that it was impossible for the Clydeshires not to have been aware why they had been invited to Ollerton.

The Earl and the Countess had stayed there on several previous occasions and they would have seen that the parties the Duke usually gave never included young unmarried girls.

But the rule had been altered, and it had in fact been his mother who had written the letters of invitation, which would have told anyone with the social consciousness of the Countess exactly why the party was being given.

The Duke thought too that the Countess, having seen her daughter's rivals, would have come to the same conclusion as he had: that she was definitely the "favourite" in the race.

'Would they, in the circumstances, really have said nothing to Lady Millicent?' he wondered to himself.

If they had not done so, that could account for the fact that she was obviously making no effort at all to make herself pleasant.

But perhaps she was so unintelligent that she actually had nothing to contribute to the conversation.

At least when he had spoken to Rosemary Castor and Alice Down during the day they had responded in a manner which left him in no doubt that they were anxious to find favour in his eyes.

The Duke was still puzzling over Lady Millicent's behaviour when the dance came to an end.

Without even smiling at him, she immediately moved to her mother's side, as was conventional, and there was nothing the Duke could do but follow her.

"I was thinking what a charming couple you made on the dance-floor," the Countess said.

"Thank you for a most enjoyable waltz," the Duke said politely.

He would have turned away, but his mother, who had been sitting next to the Countess, put out her hand towards him.

He moved quickly to her side.

"You feel all right, Mama? You must not dance if it is too much for you."

"I am enjoying myself immensely!" the Duchess replied. "I never expected to be here this evening except in a wheel-chair!"

The Duke was about to pay her a compliment when she said in a low voice:

"Can you see if Anita is all right? I have not seen her for some time."

"Yes, of course," the Duke replied. "With whom was she dancing when you last saw her?"

"With Lord Greshame."

The Duke frowned.

He had noticed that at dinner Anita was sitting next to George Greshame.

He had been invited to this particular party because he was a very good mixer, besides being an excellent bridge-player.

The Duke had thought that he would undoubtedly flirt with the two pretty, married women who had been invited.

But he had noticed that during dinner George was paying Anita too much attention, and he had thought it was a mistake.

Lord Greshame was smooth, sophisticated, and a philanderer whom most Society women did not take seriously.

He was invited to all the best parties, first because he was an unattached man, and secondly because he made himself so charming.

The Duke was aware that the women to whom he declared himself devoted laughed at his prostestations and often behind his back would say:

"Poor George! He is always seeking the *grande passion*, but after so many false starts, how can he ever hope to be first past the winning-post?"

At the same time, the Duke liked him and had thought that George Greshame would make the party, as far as he was concerned, at least tolerable.

He walked from the Ball-Room into two or three of the Ante-Rooms where a number of couples were sitting and talking, some more intimately than others.

There was no sign of Anita or of George Greshame, and he wondered if she could have been so foolish as to go with him into the Conservatory.

The girls who could be led into the Conservatory during a Ball were always something of a bad joke, but the Duke thought that Anita would not be aware of this.

The Conservatory at Ollerton, which had been erected only thirty years ago, was exceptional. Not only was it larger and better designed than most of the Conservatories attached to other houses, but it contained plants and flowers which had been brought from all over the world to make it a Botanist's delight.

There were azaleas from the Himalayas, lilies from Malaysia, and a number of plants from South America which had never been seen in England before.

The orchids were exceptional, and at Ollerton it had become customary for corsages of them to be sent to the rooms of the lady guests before dinner and buttonholes to the rooms of the gentlemen.

The Duke had noticed that Anita was wearing some small star-shaped orchids that he had thought were very appropriate on her gown, which, he was aware, was a perfect example of the type of gown a débutante should wear.

It was of white tulle which framed her shoulders like a soft cloud, and there were tiny diamantés like dew-drops scattered on it and over the full skirt.

They made Anita shimmer as she moved, and the Duke had felt, as he had noticed her dancing in the Ball-Room, that her gown made her seem as if she were illuminated with a special light.

He thought it was not her gown that people would notice, however, but the excitement in her eyes, and he thought somewhat cynically that there was at least one person who was finding the evening a joy, which was the exact opposite of his own feelings about it.

He opened the door of the Conservatory and felt the warm fragrance of the flowers hit him with the force of a wave.

Then as he moved inside he heard a little voice say:

"N-no ... please ... I want to go ... back to the Duchess!"

"I want to kiss you first," a man replied.

"I have told you ... I do not want to be kissed. Leave me ... alone!"

"You say you do not want to be kissed, but I will make you realise it can be very enjoyable, and quite frankly I want to be the first man to touch your lips."

"No . . . no! . . . Let me . . . go!"

There was a note of panic in Anita's voice, which the Duke recognised, and he moved quickly through the foliage of a large eucalyptus plant to see Anita struggling desperately against Lord Greshame, who was pulling her into his arms.

The latter saw the Duke first, and as his hold relaxed, Anita fought herself free of him.

Then as she saw who stood there, she ran instinctively towards the Duke, to hold on to him as if he were a life-line and she were drowning.

He could feel her trembling against him, but he did not put his arms round her; he merely looked over her head at Lord Greshame, who appeared to be somewhat abashed.

Then the Duke said quietly:

"My mother is asking for you, Anita."

She did not answer, she merely moved away from him without looking up and he could hear her footsteps running over the marble floor towards the door.

There was an uncomfortable silence until the Duke remarked:

"Cradle-snatching, George?"

Lord Greshame pulled the lapels of his evening-coat into place.

"A pretty little thing," he replied, "but very unsophisticated."

"Very!" the Duke agreed drily. "I therefore suggest that you leave her alone!"

Lord Greshame smiled.

"Do not sound so pompous, Kerne. Someone will teach her the facts of life sooner or later, and after all, she is only a Reader for your mother."

The Duke understood exactly what his friend implied, and it annoyed him not only for Anita's sake

97

but because he thoroughly disliked the type of man who pursued defenceless Governesses and even servants in other people's houses.

He had not thought before that George Greshame might be one of them, but now he decided that their friendship if that was what it had been, was at an end, and in the future he would certainly not invite him to any party he gave at Ollerton.

Aloud he said:

"I think you have the wrong impression. Anita Lavenham is here as my mother's guest. Her grandfather was the Earl of Lavenham and Bective and her aunt is the Countess of Charmouth."

"Good God, I did not know that!" Lord Greshame ejaculated. "I thought she had been invited to eat in the Dining-Room only to make the numbers right."

"That is where you were mistaken," the Duke replied.

As he spoke he walked from the Conservatory, not waiting to see whether Lord Greshame followed him or not.

As he walked back to the Ball-Room he realised that it was Anita's frankness that had put her into a position that she would never have envisaged.

He wondered how many other people in the house-party had thought, as evidently Lord Greshame had, that she was little more than a paid attendant on the Duchess.

As he reached the Ball-Room the Duke was wondering how he could set right what had been initiated by himself when he had saved Anita from the elderly Parson in Harrogate.

Then as the Orchestra began another of their romantic waltzes, he knew how he could make her position clear without having to put it into words.

He saw that she was already at his mother's side and he wondered if the Duchess was aware that Anita was upset.

He walked through the dancers to join them, and

he knew, as he saw the expression on his mother's face, that she was.

The Duke, however, looked at Anita.

"May I have the pleasure of this dance?" he enquired.

He saw what had undoubtedly been a terrified look in her eyes lighten, and without waiting for her to answer him he put an arm round her waist and drew her onto the dance-floor.

She was very much smaller than his other partners, but, as he had somehow expected, she was as light as a piece of thistledown, and he found that she had a natural sense of rhythm.

In fact, as they moved round the floor he had the idea that they were floating rather than dancing, and he also knew that she was still trembling a little from the fear that George Greshame had evoked in her.

"Forget what happened," he said quietly. "But let it be a lesson to you never to go into a Conservatory alone with a man unless you want him to make love to you."

Anita gave a little shiver.

"He asked me to . . . do so and I did not like to . . . refuse. When I found there was nobody else there, I knew it was . . . wrong."

"Not exactly wrong, but somewhat indiscreet."

Anita gave a little sigh.

"If Mama were here, she would have told me about . . . these things. But as you see, I am very . . . ignorant."

"You will learn by trial and error as we all have to do," the Duke said.

"I know," Anita said in a low voice, "but he . . . frightened me."

"I told you to forget him."

"I was so happy, and it has been such a wonderful experience to go to my first Ball," she murmured, "but I never expected men to be . . . like that."

"Like what?" the Duke asked, because he was curious.

"Like the Reverend Joshua, wanting to . . . marry me when he had only seen me . . . two or three times, and like . . . Lord Greshame trying to . . . kiss me when he had never . . . spoken to me until we met each other at . . . dinner."

Looking down, the Duke could see the perplexity in her small, flower-like face, and he thought that he could understand the feelings both of the Reverend Joshua and of George Greshame.

Lightly, because he felt he must stop her from becoming introspective about herself, he said:

"I think my mother would be able to tell you better than anyone else of the penalties of being a beautiful woman."

Anita was silent for a moment, then she said in an incredulous little voice:

"Are you saying . . . that you really . . . truly think I am . . . pretty?"

The Duke could not help smiling.

He was quite certain that no other man in the room to whom Anita might have asked the question would realise that she did not desire to be complimented but was genuinely and completely unaware that she was not merely pretty but lovely.

But he knew that her lack of self-consciousness, which he had noticed so often before, sprang from the fact that she was very humble about her appearance.

And when he saw her sister Sarah he had known why.

Sarah was spectacular and colourful. She was the type of English Rose who was admired as the ideal of beauty by artists of every type.

When the Duke had learnt who she was, he had thought her golden hair, her blue eyes, and her pink-and-white complexion would draw the eyes and evoke the admiration of every man in the room.

Anita was different.

She was like a small white violet for which one had to search amongst the green leaves before it was found, or perhaps a better simile was that she resembled the tiny star-shaped orchids which were pinned to her gown.

They were very rare and the Duke was exceedingly proud that he had managed to grow them in the Conservatory at Ollerton.

But he knew that the majority of people when they inspected his orchids were far more impressed by the purple Cattleya and the crimson Sophronitis and barely noticed that one which he preferred.

The answer to Anita's question was easy and he wanted her to believe him.

"I think you are very pretty," he said, "and you will appreciate that I am stating a fact, not paying you a compliment."

For the first time since they had been dancing together, the stars were back in her eyes and he knew she was no longer trembling.

"Now I am happy again!" she exclaimed. "And I promise I will never be so foolish as to go into the Conservatory again, unless there are lots of other people with me."

"And perhaps it would be wiser not to go to Church!" the Duke teased.

"I shall enquire first if the Vicar is married," Anita replied, and he laughed.

He noticed that for the rest of the evening, as he danced with his other guests, including Lady Rosemary and Alice Down, Anita was careful to return to the Duchess's side as soon as each dance was over.

She was never short of partners, and more than once as she danced past him on the floor he could hear her lilting voice talking animatedly to the man with whom she was dancing.

Sometimes too she would be laughing the gay, joyous little laugh that came spontaneously to her lips as it might have come from a child's.

In the early hours of the morning, when the

guests who were not staying in the house finally departed, the Duke said to the Duchess:

"I think, Mama, you should go to bed. I am sure your Doctors would disapprove of your keeping such later hours."

"I have enjoyed every moment," the Duchess said simply. "But Anita has already told me that I shall be very stiff tomorrow, so I will obey you."

As the Duchess spoke, Anita came running to her side, followed by two stalwart young footmen carrying a chair in which, when the Duchess had been incapacitated with rheumatism, they had taken her up and down the stairs.

The Duchess looked at it doubtfully.

"I am able to walk!" she protested.

"Not tonight," Anita said. "Please, Ma'am, be sensible, otherwise I shall have to spend all tomorrow brewing herbs."

The Duchess laughed and capitulated.

"You and Kerne both bully me unmercifully," she said, "but I suppose there is nothing I can do about it."

"Except to say good-night quickly," Anita replied. "And you know, Ma'am, you have been the undisputed and unrivalled Belle of the Ball!"

"That is true," the Duke agreed, "and I wish I had said it first!"

"It is not like you to be pipped at the post, Ollerton!" one of the guests remarked.

"I must be growing old," the Duke replied.

"That is not true," Anita said, "but just occasionally an outsider creeps in when you least expect it."

The Duke and those who were standing near were laughing as she followed the Duchess being carried from the Ball-Room.

"That is the most attractive child I have met in years!" an elderly General remarked.

The Duke thought he might say the same, but, before he could speak, the Countess of Clydeshire was gushing at him, telling him what a wonderful dance it had been.

While her mother was speaking, Lady Millicent stood at her side, and the Duke thought she was deliberately not looking in his direction, nor in fact was she making any effort to say a word of appreciation.

'The girl is a bore!' the Duke thought to himself.

At the same time, when he looked at Lady Rosemary Castor and Alice Down he knew that he could not contemplate seeing either of them at the end of his dinner-table or being obliged to present them to the Queen at Buckingham Palace.

'Perhaps Lady Millicent will improve on further acquaintance,' he thought. 'If not, I am done with her, and I will not ask her to marry me.'

Then he knew that if he did not, it would mean, as he had told Anita, more house-parties like this one; more mothers like the Countess, fawning over him in anticipation that he might become her son-in-law.

There would be more days wasted in entertaining people whom he considered bores when he might be amusing himself on the race-course, playing polo, or associating with the social crowd who circled round the Prince of Wales.

He knew that once he was married, these things would never be the same even in the case of the Prince of Wales.

At the moment the Prince never gave a party at Marlborough House to which he was not invited, and the same applied to all his married friends.

"How could we have a party without you?" Lady de Grey had said to the Duke only a few weeks ago. "You keep all the beauties on their toes in anticipation that they may be the next to catch your roving eye, and their husbands tolerate you, however audaciously you behave, for the simple reason that they know you are very well aware of your own importance and will never cause a scandal."

This was the kind of plain speaking for which the beautiful Lady de Grey was famous, and the Duke had not been offended. He merely thought as he was thinking now, that when he was married things would be different.

Of course there would be occasions when he would entertain and be entertained without his wife, but because he had a sense of propriety he knew that they would be few and far between and that as a general rule they must be seen together whenever they were in public.

He felt a wave of resentment sweep over him and decided once and for all that he would not go through with this farce to please the Queen or anybody else.

Then once again he envisaged his cousin's red and bloated face and his vulgar wife, garishly gowned and heavily over-jewelled, swaying as she walked because she had had too much to drink.

How could he allow them to live at Ollerton, to entertain at the family house in London, to inherit his other possessions all over the country?

With an effort the Duke forced a smile to his lips.

"I hope," he said to Lady Millicent, "as you do not particularly care for riding, that you will let me take you driving tomorrow afternoon? There is an attractive Folly not far from here, built by one of my ancestors, which is well worth a visit."

"Oh, what a wonderful idea, my dear Duke!" the Countess exclaimed almost before he had finished speaking. "Of course Milly would love to see the Folly."

"Then that is agreed," the Duke said, aware that Lady Millicent apparently thought her mother had said quite enough and therefore was making no effort to speak.

"Now we must all go to bed if we are to be at Church tomorrow morning," the Countess said. "I hear, Duke, that you always read the lesson."

"When I am in residence."

"Then we shall look forward to hearing you," the Countess gushed. "I am certain that you read as well as you do everything else, which, of course, is perfectly!"

The Duke inclined his head at the compliment, and then turned to say good-night to his other guests, some of whom were already beginning to yawn.

"A most enjoyable evening," they all said.

They walked towards the Hall, where there were footmen waiting for them with lighted candles in silver candlesticks which every guest at Ollerton traditionally carried upstairs to bed, even though the new gas-lighting had been installed in the bedrooms.

The Duke, who was having a word with his Butler, climbed the stairs last.

"Will you be riding as usual, Your Grace?" the man enquired as the Duke put his foot on the first step.

"Of course," the Duke replied, "and as it is Sunday it had better be eight-thirty instead of nine o'clock."

"Very good, Your Grace."

As the Duke walked up the stairs he wondered who would be riding with him, but he suspected that no-one would be energetic enough to get up early.

Then he had the conviction that that would not apply to Anita, and he was sure that his horses would be a greater draw than the comfort of her pillow.

Thinking of her reminded him that George Greshame had not said good-night but had gone upstairs before the rest of the party.

'Perhaps he is ashamed of his behaviour,' the Duke thought, 'and a good thing, too. Whoever he thought she was, George had no right to behave like that at Ollerton.'

It suddenly struck him that this was the first time in his life he had ever worried about his friends' morals, even though some of them, if he considered it dispassionately, behaved in what seemed an outrageous manner.

Because all the beauties with whom he had enjoyed his usually very ardent but brief *affaires de coeur* had been, like Elaine Blankley, promiscuous and passionate, the Duke realised that he had never thought of women in any other way.

These thoughts continued while he was undressing in silence, and when his valet left him, he got into bed and turned out the light, and found himself remembering how years ago when he had been a young man his thoughts had been chivalrous and, for want of a better word, respectful.

He recalled imagining himself as a Knight when he had sought the favour of the woman he had first loved with a reverence that was almost spiritual.

He had wanted to worship her, thinking of her as if she had the aura of a Saint and the purity of a lily.

Then, because he was so handsome and attractive, she had shown him that she was very human and desired him in a very different way.

So, naturally, he had responded. At the same time, something deep within him had told him that he was disappointed—or was it perhaps disillusioned?

He remembered how his feelings of reverence had changed to simple physical desire.

'I expected the impossible,' he thought bitterly.

Yet, strangely enough, he could remember exactly what he had felt and how the mere thought of Pauline, for that had been her name, had made him feel as if his spirit was lifted upwards, and he had wanted, because he loved her, to take the stars from the sky and lay them at her feet.

He wanted too to be finer, better, and more noble in himself; to be worthy of her.

He wanted to do great and glorious deeds so that she would be proud of him, and he thought he was ready to die in her defence and would be glad to do so.

"I was just being a fool!" the Duke told himself.

But he knew that the ideals he had sought then were still there now, beneath the surface, overlaid with cynicism and yet, strangely enough, not entirely extinct.

It struck him that if he had never met Pauline, his life might have been very different.

Then he laughed because it had all happened a long time ago, and he told himself that he was still too young to hanker after the past and what should really concern him was the future.

And his future, much as he disliked the idea, must be linked with Lady Millicent or a girl like her.

"Dammit all—there must be an alternative!" the Duke said aloud in the darkness.

But there was no answer. Only an ominous silence.

Chapter Six

As the Morning Service proceeded in the little grey stone Church in Ollerton Park, Anita was aware that Lady Millicent was praying with an intensity that she had not expected of her.

They were sitting next to each other and Anita could feel her exuding tension almost like an aura.

Anita had always been sensitive to other people's feelings and she wanted, if she could, to help Lady Millicent.

At the same time, she had no wish to intrude upon her private feelings.

The Duke read the lessons in his deep voice and Anita thought that he not only made the Old Testament and the New sound poetical but also gave the words a meaning which Parsons often failed to do.

The Service ended, and because they were in the Ollerton pew the congregation waited for them to leave first. Then as Anita reached the porch, Lady Millicent, who was beside her, said:

"Shall we walk back?"

"What a good idea!" Anita replied. "I would much rather walk than drive."

Lady Millicent told the Countess what they were going to do and the two girls set off to walk across the Park rather than down the oak-edged drive which was the route taken by the carriages.

In the distance Ollerton looked very magnificent with the Duke's standard moving gently in the breeze and the house reflected in the smooth silver surface of the lake.

"It is so beautiful!" Anita said aloud, as she had said so many times before.

Then she looked at Lady Millicent, and there was no mistaking that her pretty but usually expressionless face was filled with a look of suffering.

"What is the matter?" Anita asked. "Can I help you?"

"Nobody can ... do that," Lady Millicent replied with a deep sigh.

There was silence. Then suddenly, in a very different voice from the one in which she had spoken before, Lady Millicent exclaimed:

"I am so—miserable! I only wish I could—die!"

Anita saw that she was about to burst into tears, and, taking her arm, she drew her to where there was a tree fallen on the ground which would constitute a seat on which they could sit and talk.

By the time they had sat down Lady Millicent had her handkerchief to her eyes, although Anita was aware that she was making every effort to control her tears.

"Please let me help you," she pleaded.

"It is no—use," Lady Millicent answered in a broken voice, "Mama—says the Duke will—propose to me this—afternoon when he takes me driving—and I have to accept him."

Anita looked at her in surprise.

"You do not wish to marry the Duke?"

"No—of course not!" Lady Millicent replied. "I hate him—and I want to m-marry S-Stephen!"

Her voice broke on the name and now she sobbed uncontrollably.

"Tell me who Stephen is," Anita asked after a moment, "and why you cannot marry him."

"He is the most wonderful—marvellous man in the whole world!" Lady Millicent replied almost incoherently. "I love him—and he loves me!"

109

A burst of tears made the words almost unintelligible.

"Why can you not marry him?" Anita persisted.

"I think Papa would have agreed, in fact I am sure he would have, until the letter came from the Duchess asking us to—stay. After that he—forbade me to see Stephen—any more."

"But why?" Anita asked. "I do not understand."

Lady Millicent raised her head to look at her in surprise.

"Do you suppose Papa would miss the—opportunity of having a Duke as a son-in-law—especially one as—rich as this—one?"

"But surely," Anita said, "if your father and mother know you love someone else . . ."

"Stephen is a second son. His father, Lord Ludlow, is an old friend of Papa's, but that I love him is of no—consequence when I—might be a—Duchess."

Lady Millicent was crying once again, crying helplessly, and Anita felt deeply moved by her unhappiness.

"Listen," she said, "you must tell the Duke of this and I am quite sure he will not ask you to marry him."

"It will be too late," Lady Millicent replied. "Mama and Papa would kill me if they—thought he had asked me to—marry him and I had—refused."

"Then he must not ask you."

"How can I stop him?" Lady Millicent asked brokenly.

Anita thought for a moment, then she said:

"Shall I tell him that you are in love with somebody else?"

Lady Millicent took her handkerchief from her eyes to look at Anita in surprise before she said:

"Could you do—that? Would he—understand?"

"Of course!" Anita answered. "The Duke was very kind to me when a horrible, elderly Parson wanted to marry me, and my great-aunt, who has appointed herself my Guardian while my mother is abroad, insisted I should do so. Actually that is why I am staying here."

"And you really think he would—understand that I want to—marry Stephen—rather than—him?"

"Of course he would!" Anita replied.

She knew as she spoke that the Duke had no personal interest at all in Lady Millicent except that she was a means by which he could please the Queen and prevent his cousin from inheriting his title.

Lady Millicent clasped her hands together.

"Oh, Anita, if you can save me from—having to marry the—Duke it would be the kindest and most wonderful thing you could—possibly do for—me."

"Then I will do it," Anita said.

"It will have to be before we go driving. After all, for me to be alone with him is tantamount to a proposal before he actually asks me to be his wife."

Anita nodded.

"I understand that, and somehow I will prevent him from taking you."

"You have saved me when I thought everything was lost and I was doomed never to see Stephen again!"

"I am sure everything will be all right," Anita said.

"Mama told me before we came to Church that the Duke had said we would go driving at three o'clock. She has already decided what gown and bonnet I shall wear."

"Do not say anything to your Mama," Anita replied, "and behave quite normally during luncheon. I will speak to the Duke either just before or just after, depending on when I can get hold of him."

"You—promise you—will do—so?" Lady Millicent asked, the fear back in her voice.

"I promise," Anita answered, "and I am quite certain he will understand. He is a very understanding person."

Barbara Cartland

As she spoke, she thought of how kind the Duke had been not only about the Reverend Joshua but also in saving her from Lord Greshame.

She supposed that as Lady Millicent was so young, it had never entered his mind that she might already have lost her heart to somebody else.

In fact, thinking back over what had been said, she felt that neither the Duke nor the Duchess had thought of the three girls who came to the house on approval as people but merely as puppets to be manipulated into marriage just to suit him.

'The whole idea is wrong!' Anita thought to herself.

Aloud she said:

"Wipe your eyes, Milly, and you had better wash your face before your mother sees you. It would be a mistake for her to know you have been crying."

"I am not crying any more," Lady Millicent replied. "Thank you, oh, thank you, Anita, for being so kind to me! Perhaps if the Duke does not marry me, he will now marry Rosemary or Alice instead. I knew last night they were both hating me because he danced twice with me and only once with each of them."

Anita thought privately that neither Lady Rosemary nor Alice Down had any chance of becoming the Duchess of Ollerton, but she thought it would be a mistake to say so.

What was important was that she should save Lady Millicent, and because she was interested she asked her about the man she loved.

Because her feelings had been bottled up ever since she had come to Ollerton, they now seemed to explode and for the first time since she had arrived Lady Millicent talked animatedly and excitedly, and as she did so she looked very much prettier than she had before.

"We have loved each other for over a year," she said to Anita. "At first Papa said it was a ridiculous

112

match and he had no intention of letting me throw myself away on someone who had no chance of coming into the title."

She paused before she continued:

"Then, because Stephen was so charming to him, he had begun to weaken and we were quite certain we would be able to be married before Christmas."

"That is what will happen," Anita said with a smile.

"And you must promise me you will come to the wedding! You must be there!"

"I would love to be invited," Anita replied.

When they arrived back at the house, it was to find that it was too near luncheon-time for Anita to have a chance of speaking to the Duke before they went into the Dining-Room.

She found to her relief that she was sitting a long way from Lord Greshame but was next to a middle-aged Peer who had some excellent race-horses and they talked about his stable and the Duke's all through the meal.

When they left the Dining-Room, Anita saw Lady Millicent give her a frantic look and knew that it was imperative that she should speak to the Duke quickly, because it was already nearly half-past-two.

Therefore, she managed with some dexterity to be the last lady to leave the room, and, slipping past a number of male guests, she reached his side.

"Could I speak to you for a moment? It is very urgent," she said quickly.

He looked surprised, but he answered immediately:

"Of course, Anita. Come to my Study in ten minutes."

She smiled at him and walked after the Duchess, who was going upstairs to lie down as she always did after luncheon.

Seeing that the Duchess's maid Eleanor was there to help her onto a *chaise-longue* near the window so that she would enjoy the sunshine and the fresh air, Anita hurried down a side staircase which she knew would bring her to the Duke's Study without her having to go through the main Hall.

She had learnt that it was a room he kept for his personal use, where no-one intruded unless they were specially invited.

She opened the door and found him waiting for her, standing in front of the fireplace and looking exceedingly elegant, wearing one of his orchids in his buttonhole.

"Come in, Anita!" he said. "What is this momentous thing you have to discuss with me? I hope it will not take long as I have arranged to take Millicent Clyde out driving at three o'clock."

Anita, having shut the door carefully, moved towards him.

"That is what I want to speak to you about."

The Duke looked surprised and Anita went on:

"Milly is desperately unhappy. She is in love with somebody else and she knows if you propose to her she will be forced by her parents to marry you."

The Duke did not speak and after a little pause Anita said:

"I told her not to be upset, that you would understand and make an excuse not to take her driving this afternoon. Then her father and mother will give up hoping that they can have a Duke for a son-in-law and she will be able to marry the man she loves."

When she had finished speaking Anita looked up at the Duke with a little smile on her lips.

"I knew that you . . . " she began.

She stopped suddenly because she had seen the expression on the Duke's face.

Then as she realised something was very wrong, he said:

"How dare you! How dare you interfere in my private affairs and discuss me with my guests!"

"I . . . I am . . . sorry. . . ."

"I have never heard of such impertinence, that you should, in my own house, interfere with my plans and my arrangements. And it is utterly inconceivable that you should take it upon yourself to say what I would or would not do! Dammit all, who do you think you are!"

His voice seemed to ring out in the big room.

Perhaps because he seemed so tall and so overpowering in his rage, Anita gave a little cry of sheer fear and ran towards the door.

As she reached it, she looked back and he saw that her face was very pale.

Then she was gone, leaving the door open behind her as she ran down the passage.

* * *

The Duchess was nearly asleep when the door opened and Anita burst into the room.

"Oh, it is you, dear," the Duchess murmured.

"If you please, Ma'am, I have to leave immediately!" Anita said.

The Duchess was so astounded that she felt she could not have heard aright.

"Go—where?"

"Anywhere . . . home," Anita replied.

"What has happened? What has upset you?"

Now the Duchess was fully awake and could see that Anita was very pale and her eyes had a stricken look in them, although she was not crying.

"What has upset you?" the Duchess asked again.

"I cannot explain," Anita answered, "but please, Your Grace, let me go home. I am afraid I have no . . . money to pay the fare . . . but if you will lend it to me I will pay . . . you back."

"Yes, of course," the Duchess said. "But as it is Sunday there will be no trains so late in the afternoon. If you really wish to leave, you will have to wait until tomorrow morning."

"I would ... rather go now ... at once."

"I am sure that is not possible," the Duchess replied.

Anita gave a little sob and without saying any more turned and went from the room.

When she had gone, the Duchess rang the bell for her maid, and as the elderly woman who had served her for many years came into the room, she said:

"Something has upset Miss Anita, Eleanor. See if you can find out what it is. I am very worried about her."

"I'll see what I can do, Your Grace."

The Duchess lay back against the pillows.

There was little that went on in the house that Eleanor did not know about sooner or later, and it would be only a question of waiting before she would be informed of what had occurred.

She was not mistaken, for only a quarter-of-an-hour later Eleanor came back into the room and the Duchess looked at her expectantly.

"It appears, Your Grace Miss Lavenham went to His Grace's Study after luncheon. She was there only a few minutes before she comes out and runs across the Hall and up the stairs to Your Grace's room."

"Have you any idea what upset her?" the Duchess asked.

"No, Your Grace, but I have a suspicion that what Miss Lavenham said to His Grace caused him to send a message to Lady Millicent saying he was unavoidably prevented from taking her driving at three o'clock as had been arranged."

"Then His Grace has not gone driving," the Duchess said quietly, as if speaking to herself.

"No, Your Grace," Eleanor said, "and if you ask me, Lady Millicent must have been confiding in Miss Lavenham that she was hoping not to have to marry His Grace, being head-over-heels in love with a young man she has known ever since she was a child."

"So Lady Millicent is in love with somebody else?" the Duchess murmured.

"Yes, Your Grace. The lady's-maid to Her Ladyship's mother has been telling me, ever since they came here, how surprised they were to get the invitation, seeing as they thought Lady Millicent was to marry Mr. Stephen."

"I am beginning to understand now why Lady Millicent did not seem to be enjoying herself."

"Her Ladyship's maid tells me she cried herself sick at the idea of coming here. Believe it or not, Your Grace, it's not every young lady as wants to marry a Duke, even one as handsome as His Grace."

"So it appears!" the Duchess replied.

She had no wish to talk any more and Eleanor left her, telling her to rest and not to worry.

"Worrying never helps anyone," the old maid said, "except that it hurries one into the grave, and that's a long way off for you, Your Grace, seeing how well you've been since we returns home."

As she left the room there was, however, a very worried expression in the Duchess's eyes.

She shut her eyes and prayed, as she prayed every day and every night, that her beloved son would find happiness.

She knew he had never really been in love, and how could she explain to him how wonderful it was and that if necessary it was worth waiting indefinitely for such rapture?

Suddenly she heard the Duke speaking to somebody outside the door, and she quickly bent to pick up a newspaper which was lying on a low table beside the *chaise-longue*.

When her son came into the room she had the paper in her hand.

"Oh, Kernel!" she exclaimed before he could speak. "I am so glad you are here! Do read me this speech made by the Prime Minister yesterday. It is so badly printed that I cannot see it very clearly."

117

"Where is Anita?" the Duke asked abruptly with what his mother thought was a harsh note in his voice.

"I expect she is packing."

"Packing!"

The exclamation came from the Duke's lips almost like a pistol-shot.

"She came in a little while ago and informed me that she was leaving," the Duchess said. "She wanted to go today, but I thought it was unlikely, as it is Sunday, that there would be a train so late in the afternoon. Perhaps you would arrange for Mr. Brigstock to take her to London tomorrow. She can hardly travel alone."

Without replying, the Duke turned and left the room.

The Duchess did not seem surprised. She only watched him go, and as the door closed behind him there was a twinkle in her eyes and a faint smile on her lips.

The Duke went downstairs.

As he reached the Hall he said to the Butler:

"Send a message to Miss Lavenham to say I would like to speak to her for a moment."

"Very good, Your Grace."

The Duke walked back to his Study.

He was obviously impatient, for he walked up and down until, after what seemed a long time, the Bulter opened the door.

"I have learnt, Your Grace," he said, "that Miss Lavenham's not in the house."

"Then where is she?" the Duke enquired.

"No-one's quite certain, Your Grace, but one of the houesmaids thought, although she's not sure, that she saw Miss Lavenham running across the Park towards the Home Wood."

The Duke did not reply and after a moment the Butler said:

"I'm hoping, Your Grace, such information's in

correct, because it looks as though we're in for a
thunder-storm."

The Duke glanced out the window.

There was no doubt that the sky was overcast.

He walked towards the door and as he passed the
Butler the latter said:

"Does Your Grace require a chaise?"

"I will go to the stables myself," the Duke replied.

Five minutes later, riding Thunderer, he set off
down the drive and, having crossed the bridge over
the lake, turned towards the wood which covered a
large acreage of ground to the west of the house.

It was a wood where, the Duke knew, the trees
were thick, though it was just possible to move between them on a horse.

He guessed that Anita, being upset, would, as she
invariably did, seek a wood where she could sit and
think undisturbed.

He had not forgotten that it was a wood to which
she was going the first time they had met, when she
had been thinking of Lucifer, and a wood she was
running to for solace when she had been told that she
was to marry the Reverend Joshua.

The Home Wood was close to the house, so he
was certain that that was where she would hide
herself when she learnt that it was not possible to
leave immediately as she wished to do.

Thunderer was unusually restless and the Duke
was wondering why, seeing that he had already ridden him that morning, when a distant clap of thunder
told him the reason.

Despite his name, Thunderer disliked thunder-
storms, and looking up at the sky the Duke was sure
that the Butler had been right and there was undoubtedly going to be one, and very shortly.

He left the Park for the wood, riding Thunderer
through the trees along narrow, twisting paths covered with moss.

119

The Duke knew the wood well and he thought it unlikely that Anita would push her way through the thick undergrowth but would keep to the paths.

As he rode he was aware that except for the distant rumble of thunder, there was that quiet and stillness which came before the storm, and he hoped that he would find Anita before she got wet.

There was, however, no sign of her and he rode on and on, thinking she must have run very quickly to have gone so far in so short a time.

He calculated that it must be nearly three-quarters-of-an-hour since he had raged at her, and by moving swiftly she could have covered a great deal of ground before he could catch up.

However, there was still no sign of Anita. Then, as he was wondering if perhaps he had been mistaken and she had not come to the wood after all, he saw her.

She was in a small clearing made by the woodcutters and was seated on a recently felled tree, her head bent, her hands covering her face.

Because he had found her, the Duke instinctively checked Thunderer. Then an even nearer, louder clap of thunder made the horse start and rear up on his hind legs.

Anita looked up and when she saw the Duke she rose to her feet.

She was very pale, and her eyes, with a stricken look in them which the Duke had expected, seemed to fill her whole face.

He rode up to her.

"I came to find you, Anita," he said, "and as Thunderer hates the sound of his own name, I think we ought to get home as soon as possible."

"Yes . . . of course," Anita agreed.

The Duke reached down his hand.

She took it in both of hers and he pulled her up so that she was sitting at the front of his saddle.

She was so light that he felt as if she flew from the ground up onto the horse's back.

Then as he made to turn Thunderer there was a streak of lightning across the sky and another clap of thunder which had the horse prancing about so that the Duke found it difficult to hold him.

"Shall I walk?" Anita asked, speaking softly.

"No," the Duke replied. "There is a barn not far from here and I think we should shelter there until the worst of the storm is over."

Another clap of thunder told him that it was in fact getting very much nearer, and now the Duke forced Thunderer quickly down the path which led to the side of the wood.

With Anita in his arms it was not easy, but by a superb piece of horsemanship the Duke managed to guide the frightened animal between the trees and out into the field which was just ahead of them where they could see a hay-barn.

Even as they saw it there were the first heavy drops of rain, followed by lightning streaking its way across the sky.

Then, before Thunderer could protest, the Duke had ridden into the barn through a half-open door and a great clap of thunder sounded almost directly over their heads.

He and Anita jumped to the ground, both of them concerned only with Thunderer, who was protesting violently against the storm in the only way he knew.

It was difficult to hold him but Anita was talking to him in the soft voice she had used in the stables.

"It is all right," she was saying. "It will not hurt you. It is only a horrible noise, and you cannot see the lightning in here."

It was as if the horse was mesmerised by what she was saying.

He was tembling and moving restlessly but he was no longer rearing, and the Duke patted his neck as he held his bridle while Anita went on talking.

Then there was a noise almost like an explosion which seemed to rock the barn, and a gust of wind

121

made the door through which they had entered slam backwards and forwards.

Thunderer was still in sheer terror and Anita gave a gasp, then said in a quivering little voice:

"Oh, Thunderer ... I am frightened ... too."

It seemed almost as if the horse understood, for he turned his head to nuzzle against her, and as he did so the Duke, on the other side, realised, as if a thunderbolt had hit him, that he was in love!

He could hardly believe that the feeling which swept over him was real, and yet he knew he wanted almost uncontrollably to put his arms round Anita and hold her close so that she need no longer be frightened.

He knew too, unmistakably, irrefutably, that he wanted to comfort her and protect her not only from the thunder-storm but from anything else that might frighten or perturb her for the rest of her life.

He was astonished by his own feelings, and yet at the same time he knew that if he was honest he should have been aware of them for some time.

It was only his obstinacy and his belief that his organisation was sacrosanct which, even after he had known Anita, had made him go ahead with his plans for choosing a wife.

Now as he felt his whole body throbbing with the sudden awareness of emotions he had not known himself capable of feeling, he knew that he had loved her since the first moment she had turned her little flower-like face towards him and told him that she had been thinking of Lucifer.

He had found himself thinking of her all the time he was journeying to Harrogate, and when he saw her there it had seemed inevitable that he should find her again.

Then when he had rescued her first from the Parson and then from George Greshame, he had told himself that his motives were entirely disinterested and unselfish.

Now he acknowledged that he loved her and she

filled his whole life in a way no woman had ever done before.

There was another clap of thunder but now it was farther away, although the rain was teeming down in a torrential storm in the East and the noise on the roof made it almost impossible to hear anything else.

Anita was talking to Thunderer again and the Duke heard her say:

"It is going away. Now we need no longer feel ... afraid ... you and I, and anyway it was very ... silly of us. We are safe ... quite ... quite safe ... and we will not even get wet."

"That is true," the Duke remarked.

Anita looked at him quickly, then away again, and he knew she was shy and apprehensive that he was still angry.

They were still both holding on to Thunderer, and the Duke said:

"It is lucky that I was so anxious to apologise; otherwise you would have been soaked to the skin!"

He saw Anita's eyes flicker but she did not look at him, and he watched her face as he said very quietly:

"I am sorry, Anita. Are you going to forgive me?"

"I-it was ... wrong of me ... " she began.

"No, no!" the Duke said quickly. "You were right, absolutely right to tell me, and I will explain to you why I behaved as I did, but not at this moment."

There was silence for a moment, then Anita said:

"I ... think the rain is ... stopping."

"Hold Thunderer and I will go and look."

The Duke walked across the barn to stand at the door.

The ground was wet from the rain but the storm was dying away.

He could hear the thunder but now it was only a rumble in the distance, and as he stood there thinking that there was a throbbing in his temples and a very strange feeling in his heart, the sun broke through the clouds and the storm was over.

The Duke drew in his breath, feeling it was a sign that meant something to him personally. Then he turned and walked back to Anita.

The great stallion was eating the hay that was lying loose on the ground, and Anita in her white gown and without a bonnet looked more than ever, the Duke thought, like a small angel.

He resisted an impulse to put his arms round her and tell her how much he loved her.

He knew that she was still upset about the way he had behaved, but his love told him that he must think of her and not of himself and that this was neither the time nor the place to discuss it.

"We can go home now," he said with a smile which most women found irresistible.

"It has ... stopped raining?"

There was a little quiver in her voice which told him that she really wanted to ask something different.

"It has stopped raining," he said, "the sun is coming out, and it tells me you have forgiven me."

She did not answer and he picked her up in his arms and put her on the saddle.

Only many years of imposing a strict control over himself prevented the Duke from holding her close against his heart and kissing her. Instead he arranged her skirt and as she picked up the reins he mounted the horse behind her.

Now that the noise he disliked was over, Thunderer was behaving with the well-behaved dignity which usually was characteristic of him.

As Anita had nothing to say, the Duke was content to feel her close against his chest.

He could smell the scent she used in her hair, which reminded him of violets, and he thought that everything about her was like Spring and he knew that that was what she had brought him.

Just as last night he had recalled all the feelings of chivalry that had been his when he was young, so now he knew that Anita had revived everything that was fine and noble in his character, and he swore to himself that he would never lose her again.

Only when the house was in sight, glittering in the sunshine, did the Duke feel Anita press herself a little closer to him as if she was afraid of going back.

"Tomorrow," he said quietly, "the party will leave and you and I and Mama will be alone as we have been before."

"I . . . intended to . . . leave."

"But you will not do so because you know I want you to stay," the Duke replied. "Please, Anita!"

He could not see her face because she had her back to him, but he had a feeling that the worry had gone from her eyes.

"I . . . I will stay."

Her voice was very low, but there was an unmistakable lilt in the words and the Duke let his lips touch her hair, although she was unaware of it.

"You are mine," he said in his heart, "and I will never lose you, my precious little angel!"

Chapter Seven

The house-party started leaving early the following morning, but the Clydeshires and the Downhams were to depart at two o'clock for the station where the Duke's private train was waiting to take them to London.

During dinner the previous evening it was obvious to Anita, and she thought it must be to the Duke too, that there was an expression of disappointment on the Earl's face and a querulous note in the Countess's voice, as if they could not understand what had happened.

But Lady Millicent looked happy and was more animated than she had been at any time since she had arrived at Ollerton.

In fact, she appeared so attractive that Anita wondered if after all the Duke despite his anger, would not regret having cancelled the drive with her and having made no effort during the evening to seek her out.

The Duchess, with considerable tact, as if she realised the conversation might be uncomfortable, had arranged for a display of magic lantern slides.

Anita had found it entrancing and it was her laughter that had made the others laugh too, and the evening had therefore been an unqualified success except for the two disappointed pairs of parents.

When they had gone up to bed Lady Millicent had flung her arms round Anita and cried:

126

"You saved me! You saved me! How can I ever thank you?"

"There is no need," Anita said with a smile.

"The Duke obviously does not mind losing me," Lady Millicent remarked. "What did he say when you told him I was in love with Stephen?"

She did not notice that Anita evaded having to answer the question, nor did she know that when she went back to her own room Anita told herself it was something she never wished to think about again.

The horror of the Duke's anger still lay at the back of her mind, and the agony she had felt as she ran away into the wood was now something she wanted only to forget.

The Duke had said he was sorry when he had rescued her from the storm and had taken her back to the house on Thunderer's back, which had been an unexpectedly exciting way to travel.

But Anita still could not understand why he had been so angry.

"It is because I am merely an outsider and have really no right here in the first place," she told herself humbly. "I forced myself upon him and the Duchess, and of course it was impertinent of me to interfere in his private life."

At the same time, she felt as if her heart was singing because he had been glad that the house-party was to leave and, as he had said, they could be alone as they had been before, just the three of them.

"But how long will he stay?" Anita asked herself.

She found herself saying a little prayer that he would not be in a hurry to go back to London.

* * *

"Good-bye, Ollerton! Thank you for a very pleasant visit," the Earl said, with commendable effort.

"It has been a pleasure to have you here," the Duke replied, and to the Downhams he said much the same thing.

127

Lady Millicent kissed Anita.

"Do not forget you are coming to my wedding," she whispered as she did so.

"I shall be awaiting your invitation."

The two girls smiled at each other in a conspiratorial fashion.

Then the guests were driving away in the Duke's comfortable open carriage, while the Duchess, the Duke, and Anita waved to them from the steps.

The Duke gave a sigh that was obviously one of relief before he said:

"I expect you will want to rest, Mama."

"I am looking forward to it," the Duchess replied. "If there is one person who makes me tired it is Edith Clydeshire."

"We need not ask them again," the Duke replied, and the Duchess gave a little laugh.

She started to climb the stairs, and when Anita would have followed her the Duke said:

"I thought you would like to see a new orchid which has just arrived for me as a present from Singapore."

"A new one!" Anita exclaimed. "How exciting! What colour is it?"

"Come and see for yourself."

Anita looked at the Duchess for permission.

"Go and look at it, child," she said, "then you can tell me about it when I come downstairs for tea."

Anita smiled at her, and, with one of her little skips that showed she was excited, she walked beside the Duke along the corridor which led towards the Conservatory.

He opened the door and now there was not only the warm wave of fragrance to greet them but the whole place seemed to shimmer with a golden light because of the sun that was shining on the glass.

They walked in silence until they reached the orchids.

They all appeared to Anita to be even more beautiful and more exciting than they had the first time she had seen them.

Almost instinctively she looked for the small star-shaped one which the Duke had sent to her room the first night after she had arrived at Ollerton.

"They are all so lovely!" she said, putting out her hand to touch a petal very gently. "But this one will always mean something very special to me."

"Just as you mean something very special to me," the Duke said softly.

She felt she could not have heard him aright.

Then as she looked up at him enquiringly and saw the expression in his eyes, it was impossible to look away.

"I think you must have forgotten, Anita," the Duke said, "that I told you never to come to a Conservatory alone with a man unless you wanted him to make love to you."

"I ... I never ... thought ..."

"That it applied to me?" the Duke finished. "Well, it does! That is why, my darling, I brought you here—to tell you that I love you!"

He saw her eyes widen and a radiance sweep over her face, transforming it.

Then, as if she thought she must be dreaming, she said a little incoherently:

"What ... are you ... saying to ... m-me?"

"I am saying it in words," the Duke said, "but I would much rather say it a different way."

He put his arms round her as he spoke and very gently drew her closer to him.

Then as she stared up at him as if she could not believe that this was really happening, his lips found hers.

He knew it was the first time she had ever been kissed.

He was very gentle and he thought nothing could be more wonderful than the softness, the sweetness,

and the innocence of a kiss that was different from
any other kiss he had ever known.

Then because he could not help himself his arms
tightened and his mouth became more possessive,
more demanding.

He knew that this was what he had been seeking
all his life and had thought he would never find.

He raised his head, and when he looked at Anita
he thought that no-one who was human could look
more beautiful, more part of the Divine.

"I ... love you," she whispered.

"As I love you. Tell me, my sweet, was your first
kiss what you expected?"

"It was wonderful ... marvellous ... I did not
know a kiss could be like ... that!"

"Like what?"

"All the things I have dreamt about ... like the
moonlight ... the stars ... the sun coming through the
clouds ... and like Heaven!"

"My precious, that is what I wanted you to feel."

"Was it ... like that ... for you?"

"It was perfect and more wonderful than any kiss
I have ever known."

"Ooooh!"

He understood that there were no words with
which she could express her joy at which he had said,
and he kissed her again.

What seemed a long time later the Duke raised
his head to look down at the stars in her eyes.

"I adore you, my precious!" he said in a voice that
was curiously hoarse. "How soon will you marry
me?"

To his surprise he felt Anita stiffen. Then she
said:

"I ... love you ... and I did not ... know that ...
love could be so ... glorious ... but I cannot m-marry
you!"

If Anita had been surprised, it was certainly the
Duke's turn now.

Never had he imagined that any woman to whom he proposed marriage would refuse him.

For the moment he felt he could not have heard correctly what she said.

"I asked you to marry me, my lovely one," he said after a moment.

"I know ... you did ... and I shall always be ... very ... very ... proud," Anita said, "but I ... cannot marry you ... you must realise that."

"Why not? I do not understand!"

To his surprise, Anita moved from the shelter of his arms and turned away from him towards the orchids so that he could not see her face.

"Did I hear you say you loved me, Anita?" the Duke asked.

"You heard me ... say so," Anita replied, "and I never thought ... I never dreamt that you would love me. I think now I have ... loved you for a very long time."

"How long?"

"I think ... really since the first time ... I saw you. I thought you were L-Lucifer but that did not prevent me from loving you ... and perhaps really I loved you before that ... when I dreamt of you as an Archangel in Heaven and was worried because you fell and were unhappy ... amongst the other souls who were ... damned."

"I am not damned now," the Duke said. "I am the most blessed and fortunate man in the world because I have found you. You are everything I have ever wanted and ever longed for. Only I was so foolish in that I did not realise it at first."

He paused, then went on with a smile:

"Then I discovered that you were everything I wanted, everything that was different from any other woman I have ever known."

"That is ... why I cannot ... m-marry you," Anita said, and there was a sob in her voice.

"Do you really think I would let you refuse me?"

131

the Duke asked. "But you must explain to me why you wish to do so."

He turned her round as he spoke and saw the worry in her blue eyes and that the radiance had gone from her face.

"How can you think for a moment that you would give me up when you have said already that you love me?"

"It is because I love you so much . . . that I cannot make you . . . unhappy."

"Unhappy?" the Duke enquired. "Why should I be unhappy?"

"Because you must see I am . . . wrong for you . . . and if we married . . . I would always be waiting for the day when you would be . . . sorry you . . . had done so."

The Duke smiled.

"Do you really believe I could ever be sorry you were mine?" he asked. "I have already told you, Anita, that I love you as I have never loved a woman in my whole life, and never will again."

"B-but when you . . . look at me . . . you will be . . . disappointed."

"Are you telling me," he asked, "that you are refusing me because you do not measure up to those absurd, nonsensical conditions I set down for the appearance of the Duchess of Ollerton?"

As if she did not trust her voice, Anita nodded.

"Oh, my darling, my precious little angel," the Duke said, "do you not realise that I was being a pompous fool in thinking for one moment that one could buy a wife, as it were, out of a shop-window?"

"That . . . is what you . . . said," Anita said childishly.

"I did not know then that I would fall in love with somebody so adorable, so sweet that she fills my whole heart, my mind, and my soul, and I find her completely and absolutely perfect."

He saw the sudden light come into Anita's eyes

and for a moment she looked at him as if she reached towards him from across eternity.

Then she looked away again.

"I ... I could not ... wear the sapphire ... tiara, or the ... diamond one."

The Duke laughed and it was a very warm and loving sound.

"That is true, my precious," he said, "so we will have another one made especially for you, perhaps a wreath of flowers, or you may prefer the small halo you wear when you are acting 'as sentinel for the immortal souls.' "

Anita gave a little chuckle as if she could not help it.

"Perhaps if I am ... with you I would not be able to ... take it with ... me."

The Duke laughed before he said:

"Whether I am in Heaven or Hell, you will be with me. That is one thing of which you can be absolutely sure."

He pulled her into his arms.

"Is that your only objection to marrying me?"

"You wanted someone tall ... stately ... and beautiful like your ... mother."

"Instead I have found someone so lovely that she is in my heart and *is* my heart and nothing else is of any consequence."

Anita gave a little cry and hid her face against him.

"I love you so ... much I ... want to ... marry you," she whispered.

"And that is exactly what you are going to do," the Duke said, "and however many excuses you may find for not doing so, I have no intention of listening to them."

"Suppose," Anita said in a very small voice, "I ... make you ... angry?"

The Duke put his fingers under her chin and turned her small face up to his.

"I will tell you why I was angry," he said. "I was angry that you should have found out, as I should have found out for myself, that the girl I intended to marry was a human being with human emotions."

His voice was hard as he continued:

"When you told me that she was in love with someone else, I was shocked and disgusted that I should have just taken for granted that she would marry me, whether she wished to do so or not, because I am a Duke! I was ashamed of myself, Anita, and as a kind of defensive action I raged at you. Then when you left me, I realised what I had done."

With his lips against her forehead, he said very softly:

"I have said I am sorry and I promise I will never speak to you like that again. Do you believe me?"

"Are you quite ... quite certain you ... love me ... enough? Perhaps you should ... have another look round in case ... you find someone ... better than ... me."

"Do you think that possible?" the Duke asked. "I have to make you understand, my sweet love, that it was due to my stupidity and obstinacy, and because I am spoilt and selfish, that I nearly lost you. I will never take such risks again with you or with my own happiness. Do you believe me?"

"I want to ... desperately."

"We will be happy, my darling. I promise you that. There are so many things for us to do together; so many things about which we think the same and feel the same."

The Duke paused, then he said:

"I know that you are going to inspire me to be a better man than I have been in the past. In fact, my darling, if you will help me I feel you will not be marrying Lucifer, as you think you are, but an Archangel who has somehow found his way back into Heaven entirely because a small angel has guided him there."

Anita gave a little cry of sheer joy.

"You say such wonderful ... wonderful things to me. If you are really certain you want me ... then please ... I want ... to be ... with you and to love you forever!"

"That is exactly what you will be," the Duke said, "for our love will be eternal and even when we die we shall be together, and nothing will separate us."

He spoke in a solemn voice which Anita had never heard before, and somehow the lines of cynicism had gone from his face and his eyes were no longer mocking.

In fact he looked very different from the way he had ever looked before, and she knew it was because of love. The love she felt pulsating through her own body; the love which made her feel as if they were flying towards the sky, from which they had come.

She saw again the shaft of light which had come between the dark clouds which had made her think of Lucifer in the first place.

But she knew now that instead of him falling down from Heaven, they were both moving upwards towards the light which was all-embracing, all-enveloping.

Then, because there were no words in which to express her thoughts, she could only reach up her arms towards him, saying as she did so:

"I love you! I ... love you! I will ... try to make you ... happy."

The Duke crushed her against him.

"You have made me happy!" he exclaimed. "I love you, my precious little angel, and until the stars fall from the sky and the earth no longer exists you are mine! My angel, who has been sent to bring me a happiness I do not deserve but which I have always longed to find."

"Let me ... give it to you ... please ... please!" Anita whispered against his lips.

Then it was impossible to say any more, but only

135

to feel the sunshine overhead which had become part of them both and was burning fiercely within them, drawing them closer and closer to the heart of love, which is Heaven.

ABOUT THE AUTHOR

BARBARA CARTLAND, the celebrated romantic novelist, historian, playwright, lecturer, political speaker, and television personality, has now written well over two hundred eighty books as well as recently recording an album of love songs with the London Philharmonic Orchestra. In private life she is a Dame of Grace of St. John of Jerusalem, has fought for better conditions and salaries for mid-wives, has championed the cause of old people, and has founded the first Romany Gypsy Camp in the world. Barbara Cartland is deeply interested in Vitamin Therapy and is President of the British National Association for Health.